WHAT DO I DO?

A Tyranosaurus rex, between seven and eight meters tall, burst from the forest. Jaws gaping, it showed rows of razorlike teeth. Its tiny forearms twitched. When its black eyes focused, it let loose a horrible roar.

For the first time in many years, I knew fear. I couldn't think, could scarcely breathe.

"Roy," whispered the colonel, "what should we do?"

Robert Silverberg's
Time Tours

THE DINOSAUR TRACKERS

by
Thomas Shadwell

A Byron Preiss Book

HarperPaperbacks
A Division of HarperCollinsPublishers

This novel is dedicated to
Tim Sullivan,
dinosaur expert extraordinaire.

HarperPaperbacks   A division of HarperCollins *Publishers*
10 East 53rd Street, New York, NY.Y 10022

Cover Painting by Kevin Johnson
Interior illustrations by Alex Nino
Edited by John Betancourt
Logo and cover design by Fleming Hays Group, Inc.
Book design by Michael Goode
Special thanks to Dan Weiss, Susan Kitzen, Chris Fortunato, and Art Cover.

First printing: April 1991
Printed in the United States of America

10 9 8 7 6 5 4 3 2 1

Dear Time Traveler,

You have entered the now-time of 2061.

When time travel was discovered, fifty or so years before, the powers-that-be decided to make time traveling a tourist business. After all, you can't have people wandering around on their own, changing history— think of the effect on the future!

To begin, you must sign up for a tour at one of the Time Tour Travel Stations. Which tour do you want? The Roman Empire? The U.S. Civil War? The Prehistoric Era?

After you choose, you're outfitted in the appropriate costume of the era. Next you're given a hypno-sleep course in whatever language you may need. Finally you snap on your Time Belt and meet the Time Courier, who will lead your tour.

The Courier wears the Master Belt, which controls your belt. So don't go try jimmying your mechanism and slipping away . . .

What happens if you do? Well, there's an organization known as the Time Patrol to police such things. And if they catch a tourist or Courier monkeying around with the past, the penalty is swift *and* permanent. They may edit *you* out of history!

So have fun . . . and be careful.

Time Service Management

Chapter One

"**La**-dies and *gen*-tle-men!" The announcer's voice blared from the stadium loudspeakers. "Pre-*sen*-ting the man you've all come to see—you know who I mean—none other than *the* greatest trick rider, *the* most daring bulldogger, and *the* grandest lassoer in the whole state of Texas! That's right, three-time National Rodeo Championship winner, the rootinest, tootinest rodeo cowboy of them all. The *one*, the *only*, Roy Anikulapo Jones!"

As if on cue, the crowd went wild, hooting and hollering as only a hundred thousand lungs can. They stomped the bleachers and clapped their hands, whistling and calling my name with all their might.

I felt a hundred kilometers tall as I stood up in my horse's stirrups. Slowly I waved my white ten-gallon Stetson hat at the crowd. Then I nudged Trigger, my golden palomino stallion, into the ring. *Show time!*

The floodlights felt bright and hot as we moved forward. Their glow softened the glitter of stars in the clear night sky overhead, and I took another look at the audience. They loved me!

Then Trigger shook his golden mane, reared up, and neighed. If my horse had been born human, he would have been the greatest rodeo star of all time. As it was, Trigger had to settle for being the greatest *horse* of the greatest rodeo star.

Naturally I was as anxious to live up to folks' expectations—and more! My rodeo buddies had promised to throw Trigger and me a few surprises tonight. My buddies were good sports, but they always tried to get the best of me.

I couldn't wait to meet their latest challenge. Maybe they had a monster bull for me to ride or rope. Or maybe they had flown in some fancy Indian or Japanese sharpshooter to challenge my skill with pistol or rifle. Whatever, I was confident I could more than take care of myself. After all, I had time, experience, and Trigger on my side.

In my fanciest frilled shirt, freshly pressed chaps, and brand new shiny boots with lots of fancy silver decorations, I looked every bit the star. I had a reputation to live up to.

A wrangler signaled from my left: I'd be roping first. I nodded.

Taking my lasso from the saddlehorn, I performed a few warm-ups, twirling the loop to my right, then my left, and then up and down over my head. The gag was nothing, really; I could have done it in my sleep. But if I had thought the crowd had gone wild before, I was sorely mistaken. Their previous outburst had been just a warm-up to the cheers they now laid upon me.

Then a gate sprang open on my left, and a calf

darted into the ring. This was the start of my official routine. The calf was a scared little critter. It ran into the middle of the corral. Trigger and I were already barreling down its way. It took off like a shot—even though it had no place to go.

Hooves pounding, Trigger brought me close. I let fly with my lasso. My toss was perfect.

Everything tends to slow down during the most dramatic rodeo moments, and I saw it in slow motion. The rope cut through the air like a hot knife through butter. Its loop spread outward, slowly dropping toward its target.

Trigger came to a stop. He didn't need a signal from me; he always knew what to do.

And then the panic-stricken calf stuck its head through the lasso. Swinging from the saddle, I tugged the rope and brought the calf around. I had him on his back, legs roped together, quick as you please. Heck, I had that sucker hogtied so fast, I moved like a blur even to myself.

The crowd grew quiet. Trigger snorted at my back.

I turned to the judges' stand. I couldn't see them; black glass hid them from view, but I knew they had their heads together and their mouths working overtime. They would get the results of my little display of rodeo skill to the announcer as quickly as possible.

It must have been quite a display, even by my standards, otherwise the crowd wouldn't have been so quiet. Indeed, everyone was utterly, breathlessly silent.

"It's incredible, folks!" the announcer suddenly burst out. "Jones has done it in only *five seconds!* It's a new world's record! It's—it's *fantastic.* Almost *unbelievable!*"

But not as unbelievable as the din that assaulted Trigger and me next. I doffed my Stetson and took a bow. At my signal, Trigger shook his golden mane and took a bow also. Like I said, he was a genuine showman.

Suddenly, I got this funny little feeling up my spine, like a shiver, only different. A nagging sixth sense came to life and wouldn't leave me alone. I had a notion the surprise my buddies had cooked up for me was about to reveal itself.

Trigger nudged my back. Slowly, I turned.

A buzzer went off in my ear. It sounded like someone had inserted a buzz saw in my brain. Reluctantly I opened my eyes, reached across the arm of my easy chair, and switched off the mind-tape. The sights, sounds, and smells of the rodeo vanished. I was back in my apartment, where my body had always been.

The buzzer was my computer's alarm. A message blinked on its holographic screen: YOU'RE GOING TO BE LATE FOR WORK!

I pushed the mind-tape player away. The rodeo would have to wait until another morning. If I didn't hurry, I was going to miss the start of my first solo time tour.

Even though I liked my job, I couldn't help but sigh inwardly. The only way I was in danger of ever becoming a rodeo champ was through mind-tapes. They were the latest craze, better than video tapes by far. You not only got sight and sound, but smell, taste, even the illusion of *touch*. Just close your eyes and you are there, in the tape.

I gulped a glass of orange juice, then ran for the door. I'd have to catch the next travel pod from Under Las Vegas to make it to New Houston on time.

New Houston.... I grinned to myself. Perhaps I'd see a real rodeo tonight, after work!

Chapter Two

My mother was originally from New Dallas so I'd been to Texas plenty of times before, even lived here for a few years when I was younger. Heck, my friends in Under Las Vegas used to call me Cowboy 'cause of my Texas-twang accent. So when the pod reached New Houston and I saw the flat, open countryside studded with towering steel buildings, it felt like coming home.

One particular building, black and six-sided, loomed higher than all the rest. It was the New Houston Time Service building, of course. A blinking neon sign jutted over its roof:

IT'S THE ULTIMATE IN REALISM!
NEW HOUSTON TIME SERVICES
BRINGS YOU TO THE PAST *FASTER—
LONGER—BETTER—***AND FOR LESS!***
SATISFACTION GUARANTEED!
*ASK ABOUT OUR FREQUENT TRAVELER
DISCOUNT PLAN!*
DON'T LEAVE THE PRESENT WITHOUT US!

It took ten minutes to walk from the tube-train station to the Time Service building. Along the way I did nothing but think about my new job. My biggest concern was my first assignment. I was hoping for the Wild West, naturally. Texans are renowned throughout the Time Tour Service for their desire to experience the history of their land in the most personal way possible—by having shooting matches with Calamity Jane, getting their teeth worked on by Doc Holliday, or playing poker with Wild Bill Hickcock.

Finally I reached the Time Service building. Real marble steps led up to huge doors three times my height. They stood open, so I joined the throng of tourists headed in.

The lobby was as big as a football field, so tall you could scarcely see the ceiling. It was packed. Loudspeakers blared, alternating between country music and paging people for tours.

You wouldn't believe the crowds in front of the information booths, and sales were booming at the ticket counters. Signs blinked everywhere: "See the Alamo!" "300 Years in Three Days!" "Pancho Villa Special!"

Finally I noticed a small door marked "Employees Only." That was me, so I went through into a smaller, but no more relaxed room. Couriers in old-time western attire bustled here and there, spurs jingling on their boots. Vidphones rang constantly. Hot, overworked computers spat out reams of paper against the far side of the room. All the while, men and women talked and shouted orders at each other from every direction. I'd never seen such a mess.

The receptionist, a small black woman, looked up at me and said, "You there! Are you Roy A. Jones? The new Time Courier?"

I gave her my best grin. "Yes, ma'am!"

"You're late. Ms. Jenkins has been expecting you." She slapped a sheath of papers into my hand. "Health and dental forms. Fill them out and bring them back to me when you get a chance. For now, see Ms. Jenkins. First door to the right."

I hurried over to Ms. Jenkins' office. Inside, a very pretty blond woman of perhaps twenty-five sat at a cluttered desk, scribbling something on a pad of paper. She had a square jaw, a dimpled chin, and sharp blue eyes. Her blue and white shirt had silver spangles and a fringe along the sleeves.

When I knocked, she waved me forward. "About time, Jones," she asked. "I have a file here somewhere ..." She rummaged around on her desk and finally came up with a manila folder with my name written on it. "Here we go. Let's see, your office is in sub-basement four. You'll have a few minutes to get settled before your first tour group arrives for its briefing. They're scheduled to be here at 10:05."

"This *morning?*" I asked.

"The information is in the folder." She handed it to me. "If you have questions, I can spare five minutes."

"Who's going to be showing me the ropes?"

"Nobody. You're the only Time Courier accompanying this tour."

"But it's my first time out as a Courier. I thought regulations said an expert had to accompany me my first three trips?"

"It's in the folder, Roy. You've been bumped up a grade in the Time Service because of all the advanced time-theory courses you took in school. Besides, you've been in the past dozens of times as a tourist, so you know the ropes. You're as well prepared as any Courier in the field, theoretically. Besides, where you're going, you'll be more of an expert than anyone we could bring in on such short notice."

"Where am I going?" I asked uneasily. I'd taken a lot of history courses, mostly on Texas, but I still didn't know more than an experienced Time Courier.

"You know the new tours we're supposed to start next month?" she asked.

My uneasiness turned into a bad feeling inside. "Dinosaurs, wasn't it?"

"That's right. Well, management has been flooded with orders for the dinosaur tour. So many orders that the tours have to start immediately. It's a real problem because, as you saw on your way in, we're doing record business, and adding more tours is going to put an added strain on everyone. So we're skimping wherever possible, and making do as best we can."

"I don't understand," I said. "What's that got to do with me?"

"If we don't have at least one dino tour out by this afternoon, headquarters threatened to send us back a few days into the past to help our earlier selves get started—and devil take the time paradoxes."

"They were exaggerating, of course."

"Of course they were! They wouldn't risk the problems. But it shows how serious they are to even threaten it. So, you'll be leading our first dinosaur tour solo."

"You forgot one thing," I said. "I'm not going." I stood and tossed my folder back on her desk. My fists clenched as I remembered the dinosaur that had killed my father. "I don't *like* dinosaurs," I said. "I *hate* dinosaurs. I never want to see another dinosaur as long as I live!"

"Roy, I know a dinosaur killed your father. I'm sorry. But that was a long time ago."

"I was *there!*" I said. "I was a kid, but I wanted to be a paleontologist like Dad. When I was twelve and on a research trip with him, he came too close to a Tyrannosaurus rex. *It ate him.* Right in front of me. *It ate him!*"

"I'm sorry," she said.

"And do you know what else?" I said. I couldn't keep the bitterness from my voice. "Because it was one of the first trips back that far, the Time Patrol wasn't allowed to interfere. They could have gone back and stopped Dad from taking the trip, but they wouldn't. They said he was *meant* to be eaten, and saving him might change history."

"Roy," she said softly. "I'm sorry your father's dead. But that was six years ago. It's time to get on with your life."

"I don't need a lecture!" I told her.

"Then perhaps you need a little reminder. In case you've forgotten, you signed a contract with the Time Service. That contract says you'll work wherever and whenever we assign you."

"I was promised historic Texas!"

"You'll still be in historic Texas, Roy, only a few hundred million years earlier than you'd thought. There's nobody else here with any knowledge of dinosaurs or the Mesozoic era. If this tour is going to succeed, *you* have to guide it. We *need* your expertise."

"I'm sorry," I said softly. "I can't."

She sighed and shook her head. "Then I'm afraid I'm going to have to exercise clause 33-j in your contract. It says, 'If the Courier knowingly, deliberately, and/or maliciously fails to guide an authorized tour assigned to him, he shall be held personally responsible for all fees due to Time Services, Inc., and his contract shall be terminated forthwith.' "

The lump in my throat threatened to choke me. "So I'm fired?"

"After you pay—" She rummaged around on her desk again. "Let's see, it's 15,430,000 credits for this tour."

I yelped.

"Will that be cash or charge, Roy?"

"That's blackmail!"

"Just good business sense."

"I think," I said slowly, sitting down again, "that I've reconsidered." I hated giving in to her, but I didn't have much choice. There were scarcely fifteen credits in my bank account—let alone fifteen million. And I needed the job; I'd studied for this for the last two years of my life.

"Yes?" she said.

I glared. "I'll take the tour. But I'm not happy!"

"You get a bonus when you return because certain unspecified dangers come with the territory."

"Nice." My tone was sarcastic. "And what happens if one or more of my tourists gets killed or eaten?"

"They won't. Not if you do your job right."

"But we won't know that until *after* the tour!"

"If some mistake is made, I'm sure the Time Patrol will fix it. Unless, of course, it's that person's destiny to die during the reign of the lizard kings. Once you've introduced yourself to your tour group, I'm sure you'll feel better. There are still a few more surprises for you. Pleasant ones, I hope."

"Why do I doubt it?"

Chapter Three

"Yee-haa! Let's hog-tie them suckers!"

I had never expected to hear those words echoing through the thick, sultry forests of the late Cretaceous period. Of course, generally speaking, I'd never dreamed that as a Time Courier, I'd be escorting a passel of bronco busters to the Mesozoic era.

One Perry Owens, known to friend and foe alike as "Deadshot" Owens, balanced atop a ridge while a pack of dromiceiomima stood in a dry gully below and stared up at him with large, black eyes. Droms (as we called them) looked like a cross between a featherless ostrich and a hairless horse, and were at least as big as the latter. They ran on two powerful hind legs and had thin arms equipped with tiny clawed digits. Their arms, along with their tails, helped them maintain their balance. Their heads were so small their brains must've been the size of walnuts.

Deadshot, on the other hand, was a bowlegged barrel of a man. His long blond hair blew in the breeze. His moustache had been twisted and waxed until stiff. He chewed tobacco and spat the juice twenty paces every time.

The droms clearly didn't know what to think of Deadshot. They poised, ready to run if he threatened them.

"Yee-*haaa!*" Deadshot shouted again. He pulled rope from his belt, twisted it into a lasso, and began twisting it over his head.

The droms didn't like that. They suddenly bolted, raising a huge cloud of dust. Deadshot gave chase, skidding down the ridge and into the gully after them.

"Hey!" I shouted after him. "Leave them alone! *Deadshot!*"

He didn't hear me, or pretended not to. Earlier I'd told him he could watch droms all he wanted, but couldn't do anything else yet without my permission. We had more important things to do first, like getting our camp fortified against predators. If I had to visit the age of dinosaurs, I had no intention of letting what had happened to my father happen to me.

Now, as Deadshot vanished from sight up the gully, I cursed to myself. I *knew* I shouldn't have trusted him. Like all western cowboys, he had no regard for authority.

I scrambled down the hill where we'd made camp, running straight for where I'd last seen him. The rest of my tour followed right on my heels. I knew I had to stop Deadshot. If he interfered with the course of time or if the droms or some other dinosaur hurt him I'd never hear the end of it.

We reached the ridge in time to see him corner three young droms several hundred meters down the gully. The little dinosaurs were making helpless braying noises, looking for a way past him.

"Deadshot!" I shouted, horrified. "Don't!" I turned toward the tall, fat tourist standing beside me and said helplessly, "He promised he wouldn't do anything!"

The tourist smiled and shrugged. "He lied." The tourist was Colonel Tom Maynard. I don't know how or where he'd earned the rank of colonel, but I'd learned long ago never to argue with a man who eats three steaks for breakfast.

Deadshot threw his lasso. The loop soared toward one of the long drom necks, but the dinosaur ducked out of the way.

The others let out whoops of encouragement. Deadshot grinned as he reeled in the rope for another try.

"That's great," I said sarcastically. "So what am I supposed to do if he breaks the drom's neck and changes history?"

"Son, you're a wild one!" exclaimed the colonel, slapping me between the shoulder blades. My backbone felt like a pack of cards thrown in the air. "Dinosaurs can't change history!" he said between guffaws. "They're all gonna die anyway!"

He was referring to the legendary comet that would hit the Earth in just a few million years. When the comet struck, its impact threw millions of tons of dust into the stratosphere. The dust orbited the Earth for years, blocking the sun's rays. Without light, the Mesozoic jungles died. And without their food supply, the dinosaurs soon became extinct.

Being made of ice, the comet shattered on impact and left only microscopic traces. Its existence hadn't even been suspected until the twentieth century. Before then, the extinction of the dinosaurs had remained a mystery.

Even if the dinosaurs *were* all going to die, I couldn't permit the colonel's casual attitude toward time paradox (however unlikely) to pass without comment.

"Yeah," I said, "but maybe one of those critters is fated to eat a plant that would otherwise begin an evolutionary trail toward, oh, I don't know, intelligent plant life or something."

"Maybe, son. But your supervisor said any alterations in history this far in the past would average out anyway. It's the latest wrinkle in paradox theory. I seem to recall that you were standing there while she said it."

Yes, Louise Jenkins had said that all right. But I didn't like it very much.

"Besides," continued the colonel, "Deadshot's just practicing on a few dumb varmints. Ain't nothing going to happen to 'em. It ain't like he's gonna hogtie some general or philosopher. Though I tell you, if we stumble across Cleopatra or Helen of Troy, or any of them other great historical beauties, you'd better watch out for Deadshot and me both!"

I tried to relax. Deadshot's second and third efforts to lasso a drom also proved duds. He wasn't living up to his name.

Then my heart leaped into my throat. "No," I groaned.

Deadshot's latest effort was in mid-throw, but you could tell it was going to succeed. The rest of the crew let out shouts of triumph. And sure enough, Deadshot's lasso slipped around a drom's neck.

Deadshot yanked the rope. When it tightened, the drom let out a startled screech and took off like its tail was on fire.

Deadshot braced himself, looping the rope around his wrist, but the drom jerked him off his feet like he wasn't even there. It kept on going, dragging him after it. Deadshot hooted in delight. Then the two of them disappeared behind a hill.

"Wish I had my dog here," the colonel said. "He'd round that varmint up." Then he pulled his old-fashioned six-gun from his holster and fired a slug into the air. "Charge!" he shouted.

And then he and all the others ran to the next ridge and disappeared down the gully in search of their compadre. I just stood there, dumb as a star lummox, feeling disgusted and slightly jealous my tour was having fun in what was, for me, a miserable era.

Now I know what some of you must be thinking: that it isn't customary for a Time Courier to permit his clients unsupervised liberties. But in this case—and in all similar incidents in the future, as Louise Jenkins had already explained to me—it was jake with paradox theory, thanks to the exorbitant fees the Time Service had accepted from my clients' sponsors, the Texas Rodeo Association.

That explained why they'd paid fifteen million credits for a tour that should (in my estimates) have cost no more than a few hundred thousand. That also explained why I didn't just end the tour then and there and drag them all back to the present for disobeying me. I'd been ordered to look the other way if anything out of the ordinary happened . . . as long as it didn't interfere much with history.

Louise had certainly stuck me with a motley crew of wild-West show-biz eccentrics. Deadshot and the colonel weren't the only characters. Next came Ziggy Stone, a Jamaican bronco-buster who had a ring through his right nostril and a pair of tiny bells dangling from his left ear. Ziggy wasn't too bright—the result of having landed on his head too many times.

Next came Kansas Alice. Alice was a double-rig semi of a female, big, beefy, and wide. According to her file, she had begun life as a sweet, tiny thing. But she had so admired Calamity Jane that she had had her entire body surgically altered to resemble that big sharpshooting heroine of the days of yore. Having seen Calamity Jane in the flesh a couple of times, I must admit that the surgeons had done a good job on Alice. Of course, the real Calamity Jane hadn't had a cybernetic eye for sharpshooting, but no one had ever expected her to hit a half-credit coin five hundred meters away with a laser derringer.

Then there was Elroy Higgins, better known to his friends as Wylde. Wylde was the bravest and most effective clown on the modern circuit. The typical rodeo clown uses his comedic talents as a tool to distract an irate horse or bull and keep it from stomping on a fallen cowboy. And he still must get laughs. Wylde was the best, and he had the records to prove it.

And I couldn't forget Joan Wesley Hardin. That's right, Joan Wesley Hardin. As a teenager, she'd been a major part of the famous "Dickie Don't Singing Platypus Club" vid show. Dickie was a cartoon character who was supposed to be the star, but it was the youthful Joan who, with her cowgirl outfit and her plastic platypus beak tied around her head, was the heartthrob and first pin-up girl of zillions of boys. She had worn that platypus beak even while she played the guitar, sang country-western tunes, and demonstrated her considerable skills as a trick rider. She still wore the same sort of cowgirl outfit, though cut for a more adult figure now.

And she still had talent. In addition to being a vid star, she was a world-class champion trick rider, and easily turned out a couple of hit country-western songs a year. Just thinking about her sent me to the moon.

"What a bunch of dweebs," said the female voice behind me.

My hackles rose like the pins on a porcupine's back. In all the excitement I'd forgotten all about Mallory Byrne. I wondered how I possibly could have forgotten her, even for a moment. When we'd met in my office earlier that morning, three hours earlier in elapsed time, when we were still in 2061, I hadn't liked her at all. She'd been very cold, and she'd rubbed in all the wrong ways.

"Funny," I said, glancing over at her, "I would

have thought Ms. Hardin would be the snob of the outfit."

"Because she's the biggest star?" Mallory Byrne gave a snort of contempt. Then she smiled. It took quite an effort, I could tell, because the expression in her eyes implied she would like to feed me to the pterosaurs. She offered me her hand. "We didn't get much of a chance to talk earlier, Roy. You can call me Mallory."

"Thanks." I shook her hand suspiciously. I had the feeling she wasn't introducing herself to be polite, but because she wanted something from me, something she wasn't ready to ask for yet. *What?*

"I guess you know all about me already," she said.

"Just what was in your file. You're an honors graduate from the Harvard Temporal Law School. You've had several papers regarding paradox theory published in leading journals. You wrote one on the rights of time tourists that won an award somewhere. It was quite good, actually."

"You've read it?"

I nodded. "Required to at school."

She smiled. "All that's ancient history, as it goes. After I graduated from Harvard, I became a reporter."

I slapped my forehead. "You're *that* Mallory Byrne! Of course! You used to work for the American HoloVision Network. You broke the story about rogue bankers laundering gold and silver through banks in the nineteenth and twentieth centuries."

"That's right," she said proudly. "I got an exclusive on the temporal money-laundering scandal."

"Then you disappeared from the air. What happened?"

"I got fired," she said, shrugging without a trace of regret. "It happens all the time. You stick your nose where it doesn't belong, you embarrass somebody important—"

"Your ratings hit the dumper," I put in.

She winced. "And you get fired. I could have worked elsewhere in the news business, but I wanted to do something else for a while."

"So you became a cowgirl?"

"That's right."

"That's kind of difficult to believe."

"Not if you get to know me." My expression must have revealed what I was thinking (*Not a chance, lady!*) because she added, "Anyway, my folks rode the circuit. My entire extended family did, really. When Mom and Dad got too old for the physical parts of rodeo, Mom became a sharpshooter and Dad trained and managed hot young cowpokes. So you see, I was raised with a bridle in one hand and a laser derringer in the other. In fact, on my better shooting days I can disintegrate an apple on a wooden Indian's head at a hundred meters. Want to try me?"

"Not really."

That brought her up short. "Well," she began, "I ... I just wanted you to know that I realize I wouldn't have gotten anywhere without the hard work and sacrifices my parents made. That's why it means a lot for me to be part of this outfit."

That sounded about as sincere as a coyote

sweet-talking a prairie dog. "Just what do you want from me, Ms. Byrne?"

"Why—I—nothing! I want nothing from you! Not even the time or the year!" With that she turned and stalked toward the gully after her fellow tourists and Deadshot.

Much as I didn't like her, I still had a job to do. After all, when I'd become a Time Courier, I'd sworn an oath to "Bring 'em back alive!" So I too went down the ridge and into the gully.

Dust from the droms' stampede was settling over the trail Deadshot had left when the little dinosaur had dragged him. We followed the trail around twists and turns, over rocks and several fallen logs. Several times I saw dark spatters of blood. It was Deadshot's, I felt certain.

"Don't worry," said Mallory. She had slowed down so I could walk beside her. "Deadshot's been cut worse. Besides, Wylde always carries a portable med kit. And we have full medical supplies back at the camp."

We hiked until the gully opened up into a relatively flat plain. There we found the rest of the cowpokes standing around, looking at a hogtied drom. The dinosaur lay on its side, bleating softly.

I had to admire Deadshot's determination. He'd taken what must have been a pretty terrifying trip through the gully without letting go of the rope. Further, the moment the drom had stopped, he'd gotten up, wrestled it to the ground, and come out on top. That's a *real* cowboy for you!

As Deadshot sat on a rock, Wylde applied salve

to his rope-burned hands. Deadshot's every movement seemed to hurt, and I wondered if he might not have a couple of cracked ribs beneath his tattered, blood-stained clothing. Despite his pain, though, he was as happy as a clam.

"Okay," I said to him, "I'm impressed. You've proved you can rope a dinosaur. What say we let the little critter get back to the rest of his herd?"

Deadshot looked up. "Can't do that," he said.

"Why not?"

He laughed. "I haven't ridden him yet!"

I looked at Wylde. "Is he up to it?"

"Sure," the rodeo clown said. "His hands are almost healed now, thanks to this here miracle goo, and there doesn't seem to be much else wrong with him."

Frowning, I nodded. "I guess it can't do any more damage. Go for it!"

Deadshot gave a whoop. "Saddle him up! *Hoo-weee!*"

When the lot of them began talking about how to cinch saddles around a dinosaur's most unhorse-like chest, I just shook my head.

It took a couple of hours to get everything ready. Wylde and Kansas Alice had to lug a pair of saddles from our camp: one western style and one English to see which one would work best. In the meantime, Ziggy, Deadshot, and the colonel managed to lasso another drom when it strayed too near. With three of them holding on, it didn't stand a chance.

"Which one should ride first?" Deadshot asked.

"Ride your own," Joan Wesley Hardin retorted. "I saw this one first!"

Suddenly she ran straight for critter they'd just caught. She jumped on its back, knotted makeshift bridle and reins out of her rope, and slipped them over drom's head.

And that's when the drom let out a terror-drenched sound somewhere between a yell and a moan. Then it concentrated on bucking Joan from its back.

Joan dug in her heels and hung on for dear life.

Chapter Four

"This is crazy!" I exclaimed, suddenly realizing the danger. "Nobody's ever ridden a dinosaur! Nobody even knows if their temperament is vaguely like ahorse's! She's going to get herself killed!"

But I didn't have anything to worry about. Joan stayed on the drom's back. The drom couldn't kick up its hind legs like a horse because its arms were too short and stumpy. So instead it shjook its back like a dog shaking off water. That sounds innocent enough, but if you have the strengthy of a dinosaur, even a comparatively little one, it can be quite a ride! Joan's teeth clacked like an angry rattlesnake's tail.

Next the drom tried running in circles at the same time, but that didn't work, either. So, in desperation, it knelt and tried to roll.

Ziggy ran around and yanked the critter's head in exactly the opposite direction with his lasso. This maneuver prevented it from getting a single knee to the ground, but it tried again and again. So Ziggy had to fight to keep the critter upright just as hard as Joan had to fight to stay on.

But she stayed on.

"Well, what do you know?" said Mallory, beaming proudly. "I believe this idea of mine is going to work after all!"

"What idea?" I asked.

"Why, this whole trip," Mallory said proudly. "The whole idea of a dinosaur rodeo."

"A what?"

"A dinosaur rodeo!" she said, with the light of capitalism firing up her eyes. "Think of a stadium full of people coming back to the Mesozoic Era for the greatest show of all time!"

Exhausted, Joan's drom sank to the ground and wouldn't get up. She hopped off, beaming proudly.

"That's one for the history books!" she said. "The first person to ride a drom!"

"You robbed me," Deadshot grumbled, but he didn't seem disappointed. After all, he'd been the first to rope and hogtie a dinosaur, and he'd done it single-handed.

"A dinosaur rodeo," I repeated, dumfounded. It sounded crazy, but I liked it.

The two droms were "ours," the colonel decided. He wasn't about to let them go now, after they'd proved rideable.

"But what will you do with them?" I asked.

"Well, son, I reckon we'll just have to train 'em. Maybe teach the critters some tricks!"

I shook my head, but he was paying, after all, and had a lot more pull with the Time Service than I did. If we were changing history by capturing a few dinosaurs, the Time Patrol would just have to set us straight later.

Colonel Tom fashioned blinders and slipped them over the droms' eyes. The critters settled down and let us lead them toward camp.

"Do you need more than two?" I asked.

"Two is a good start," the colonel said. "Why?"

"They seem to like the gully, so ... maybe we could block the ends and trap a herd." I couldn't believe what I'd just said.

The colonel gave me another bone-jarring slap on the back. "That's the spirit, son! I knew you'd come around!"

Nearly three hours had passed by the time we got back to camp. As we topped the hill, I noticed forty or fifty dog-sized dinosaurs foraging among our belongings. The camp was such a mess, it looked like a tornado had struck while we were gone.

"Oh, no!" I heard Mallory groan.

I dashed forward, shouting and waving my arms. After a second, everyone joined me.

The little dinosaurs scattered, revealing the full extent of the disaster: pots and pans scattered across the hilltop, tents trampled flat, and our supposedly dinosaur-proof storage lockers smashed. Bits of walkie-talkies, medical kit, autochef, and laser rifles lay crushed among the cans and empty or half-eaten boxes of food.

"Little varmints!" the colonel said.

"Nothing we can do about it now," I said heavily. "If we'd finished putting up the camp's defenses instead of chasing droms, this wouldn't have happened."

The colonel nodded, and Deadshot studied the ground. "I guess you're right there, son."

"Next time, listen." I looked across the ruins of our camp and shook my head in disgust. "All right, let's dig in. If we work hard, we can have the camp back in shape by nightfall."

The colonel said, "It's not so bad. We have more than enough food. And we can cook over the campfire, just like cowpokes used to. Now, how about giving me a hand getting my tent back up, Roy. I don't think them varmints can eat through kevlar."

I nodded; kevlar was the next best thing to indestructible. It would take more than claws to cut through our tents.

As I helped the colonel set his tent up again, I couldn't help but notice the footprints on one side. *Human* footprints, and several sets. If we weren't millions of years away from any other people, I might have thought strangers had snuck into camp, jumped on everything, and then fled before we got back.

I supposed the colonel and I must have walked on the tent when we were setting it up that morning. The footprints *were* faint, and one set *did* seem to be my size.

And how did dinosaur-proof storage lockers get opened? I wondered. I gave the jungle around us a slow look. Nothing seemed unusual or out of place ... just us, humans in a time we were never meant to see.

I shook my head. Paranoia was getting the better of me. Of course it had been dinosaurs. They could be clever at times, couldn't they? And they were certainly full of mischief.

I concentrated on getting our camp straightened out.

To make a long story short, my tourists spent the next seven days in the Upper Cretaceous. During that time, they figured out how to tame and ride droms, practiced roping a variety of small dinosaurs, and generally had a real blast.

Luckily for the cow-punchers, Colonel Tom had studied up before the trip, and knew what sort of reward you'd offer a dinosaur for a job well done. He'd brought several thousand sugar-cube-sized "dino-treats" for just that purpose.

Without the dino-treats, and the other information Colonel Tom had, the dinosaur training would have been trial and error. And it might have resulted in a few grisly incidents.

But as matters stood, things went smoothly after our first day, and things settled into routine. Since I couldn't rope or ride, and I didn't like dinosaurs, I spent my time watching the others have a good time. It wasn't boring, but after the first few days, it wasn't much fun.

During the fifth night, after everyone else had gone to bed, the colonel built up our cooking fire until it blazed. Since nights in the Mesozoic Era are warm, we didn't really need it, but I didn't mind all that much. It kept back the darkness.

"You know, son," the colonel said, "this reminds me of the times I camped out as a boy."

"Really?" I had been idly guessing which stars would eventually reconfigure into the familiar constellations of my era. "It doesn't seem much like Texas to me."

"Not that." He gestured around him. "All of the wilderness out there. You think you're all alone in the backyard. Never mind the neighbors twenty meters away, or the street just beyond the fence. You can dream it's just you and your dog taming the unknown. Great times, son, great times."

"Great times indeed." Around us, insects chirped, clicked, and chittered. Farther out, larger beasts screamed into the night. It was a jungle out there.

Then Mallory Byrne emerged from her tent. She took one look at the campfire, then came over and sat next to me.

I'd been trying to avoid her, but she took advantage of every opportunity to be with me, whether I was interested or not.

"You know, Roy," she said, "I don't know a thing about you."

"Funny about that," I replied noncommittally.

Colonel Tom rose and stretched, giving me a sly wink. "I'll leave you two kids out here." Grinning, he headed for his tent.

"I think I'll turn in, too," I said.

"Why don't you stay?" Mallory asked. "I'd like company."

I settled back. If she only wanted company, I could stay, I reckoned.

"Have you been a Courier long?" she asked.

"Nope."

"For a little while?"

"Yep."

"This your first trip as head honcho?"

"Yep."

"Are you always so talkative?"

"Usually."

"Isn't there anything," she said sweetly, "that you would like to ask me?"

I shook my head. "Not really."

"What do you mean by that?"

"Exactly what I said. You're just a client, a tourist from the Texas Rodeo Association on a visit to the past. That's the sum total of our relationship. Period."

"Roy ..." She leaned close. I smelled a tangy perfume.

Why? I asked myself, tensing up. I still sensed a chill beneath her words, like everything she'd said had been part of an act. I knew for certain she wanted something, and she thought she needed to charm me into giving it. *What?*

"Let me tell you a secret," she said huskily.

A branch cracked, sounding like a pistol shot, and we both jumped. It was Ziggy, who'd just climbed out of his tent.

"Sorry to interrupt," he said. "Got to feed the droms."

"Great," I said, standing. "I'll give you a hand."

Mallory rose and stomped back to her tent without a word. Smiling, I followed Ziggy toward the corral.

Ziggy glanced at me and grinned. "Better watch your step, lad," he said.

"Huh? How come?"

"I probably shouldn't say anything ..."

"Tell me," I insisted.

"It's just that sometimes you need to be careful. Be careful, will you?"

Terrific, I thought. Clearly Ziggy existed on a plane separate from everyone else.

He carried a bag of dino-treats over a shoulder. Basically they were lab-grown protein bars, designed to match the fibers the creatures from this era were used to digesting. The dino-treats intended for droms were a plant derivative; for carnivores we had a meat-flavored treat.

The droms had become pretty tame. Only a few ropes hobbled their back legs and tail, to keep them from running if they managed to escape. But there didn't seem much chance of that. They liked four square meals per day, and seemed only too happy to perform for people.

When they saw us coming, they crowded to our side of the corral. With a distracted air, Ziggy opened the bag. The dino-treats' odor, like a combination of asparagus, onion, and baked beans, poured out. The droms began to shift from foot to foot, making impatient whistling noises.

Ziggy looked back and grinned at me as he took

the first treat from the bag. "Ever hear of a Jamaican cowboy before?"

"Actually, no," I said.

"I'm the only one in the world. It's strange, being around all you Texans."

He tossed a dino-treat to a drom. The critter snapped it up. The other drom strained its neck forward until it got its treat. Ziggy continued tossing them treats as we talked.

"You know," he went on, "I had to learn a whole lot about Texas and its history to fit in. All the things you native-born Texans take for granted. Like the history of the Alamo."

"I'm afraid I don't understand," I said.

"Well, shoot, son. It's just that I'm getting too old to be a wrangler much longer. I've been thinkin' about settling down. Maybe finding a wife, having kids. I was thinking … seeing as how I've studied Texas and Texans a lot, maybe you could give me some advice. How do I get to be a Time Courier?"

I laughed. "It's not hard. You go in and apply."

"That's it?" His mouth hung open.

"Well, they have tests for you to take, to make sure you know your history and you're good with people. And you're not some nut who's going to go rampaging through history with his Master Time Belt, doing stupid things like saving Abraham Lincoln from being assassinated, or setting Al Capone up with a criminal empire, or giving the Romans advanced technology."

Ziggy paused in thought. Unfortunately, he happened to be holding a dino-treat. The first drom, sniffing the aroma, stuck its neck out and chomped.

Ziggy's eyes got big and wide. His complexion paled. His mouth twitched as if to scream.

I must give the drom credit: it wasn't greedy. It didn't try to take the entire thing, just what was between Ziggy's fingers. If the critter had a brain in its head, I'm sure it would have asked, "How was *I* supposed to know Ziggy's finger was in the way?"

Ziggy yelped and spun around. He practically fell into my arms, clutching his injured hand. Thanks to the clear bright moon, I had a magnificent view of his injury. Blood spurted.

Chapter Five

"**A**re you all right?" I asked stupidly.

He mustered the strength to laugh. "Oh, my boy, you are a strange one."

"Wylde!" I shouted. "Get the med kit! Ziggy's hurt! *Wylde!*"

It might have been a fire drill, the way they poured out of their tents. They helped Ziggy over to the fire.

Then Wylde pushed through with the med kit. Alice and I held Ziggy's arm while Wylde examined the wound.

"Thank goodness, he only bit your finger off," said Wylde a few moments later.

This time Ziggy's laughter had more spirit. "Is that all?"

"Yeah. I'll bandage you up, and you can get a new finger when we get back to our time."

They both laughed, as much from nervous relief as anything else. Suddenly Ziggy groaned. "A new finger's going to cost a fortune!"

"Don't worry, son," the colonel said. "Since we're here on business, the Texas Rodeo Association's insurance company will pay for it. Heck, ain't that what it's there for?"

That night, as I lay on my cot in my tent, sleep wouldn't come. My thoughts kept turning to Mallory, the droms, and Ziggy.

These people could be plenty tough. Sure, you could get a new finger in our time, but that didn't mean losing one hurt any less. Usually the only kind of blood modern entertainers spilled was the fake kind. Deadshot and Ziggy both had handled their injuries far better than I would have.

Would they be able to pull off their dinosaur rodeo? They had spent the better part of their lives on the rodeo circuit, riding and roping and shooting like their lives depended on it. They could have stayed at home and played mind-tapes like me, but they hadn't. They worked to make their dreams real. And yes, I thought they would succeed.

In the end, I had to admit I was jealous. They were going to make history. All I could do was stand around and watch.

Finally I unsealed my tent flap for a breath of fresh air. I stood there just gazing out into the night. The campfire had died down and insects hummed in the night. I stared at millions of glittering stars set in a sky that had never known pollution.

Then a branch snapped. Instantly alert, I peered into the darkness beyond the fire's embers. A dinosaur? Or one of our dino-punchers gone for a walk?

Another branch cracked. Something was moving out there.

I found a flashlamp, flicked it onto narrow beam, and scanned our camp. Two men with laser rifles were standing just beyond the dying campfire. I didn't recognize them.

"Hey there!" I shouted. "Who are you?"

The one on the right jerked his rifle around toward me. I dived for the floor.

Something bright and hot sizzled over my head. I smelled burning kevlar.

"Help!" I shouted to the rest of our camp. "We're under attack! *Get your weapons!*"

My hand flew to my Time Belt. By feel, I punched in the code to summon the Time Patrol. I wasn't taking any chances!

Then I fumbled around on the floor until I found my flashlamp. By then the rest of my tourists were all standing around my tent, looking confused. The colonel had his six-shooter drawn, and Joan held a laser rifle. I joined them outside.

"What's going on, son?" the colonel demanded.

Quickly I told them what had happened.

"Sounds like quite a dream," said Joan.

"That was no dream!" I pointed out the two neat little burnholes in my tent. "Those two shot at me, all right."

"I guess they surely did." She looked worried, suddenly, and glanced around at the darkness surrounding our camp.

"They'll be long gone," Colonel Tom said grimly. He threw more wood on the campfire. "Ain't no cause to panic. We'll set a watch. Tomorrow morning we'll find their camp."

I shook my head. "I'm afraid not. This isn't something we can deal with. I've called the Time Patrol, and they should be here soon."

There were protests, but I held up my hands.

"I insist," I said. "I've overlooked lots of ... *irregularities* on this tour so far. But attempted murder is too much. Besides, this is the second time they've been here. Who know what will happen if they come back again?"

"What do you mean, the second time?" the colonel demanded.

I told him about the footprints on his tent the first day we'd been here, when our camp had been torn up. "I decided I had to be imagining things," I said. "But there *are* other people in this time period. And they're not friendly."

The air suddenly shimmered by the campfire. A pair of men in black Time Patrol uniforms appeared, laser pistols drawn. They glanced at the dark jungle, then headed toward us.

I stepped forward. "I'm Roy Jones, the Courier."

"Captain Fredericks," the man on the left said. He was tall and thin, with short-cropped blond hair and an upturned nose. He nodded to the short, stocky man beside him, with curly black hair and a dark complexion. "My partner is Lieutenant Einar. What's wrong? Did you lose one of your tourists?"

"Of course not," I snarled. "I'm *trying* to report an attempted murder!"

That got his attention. "Let's find someplace more private to talk," he said, more businesslike suddenly.

I led the way to the far side of the camp. The colonel followed, but Fredericks didn't object.

"Okay," Fredericks said. "Let's hear it."

Quickly I outlined my encounter with the two men, and I pointed out the laser-burn holes in my tent. Then I told them about our camp being wrecked our first morning here.

Fredericks was nodding. "I'm afraid you've run into bootleg meat-runners," he said.

"See here," the colonel interrupted. "Bootleg meat-runners? I ain't never heard of them varmints before."

"We're trying to keep it quiet," Einar said. "It seems someone is going back in time, slaughtering dinosaurs, and peddling their meat in the twenty-first century. We haven't been able to capture them."

"There you go," I said. "They're here, in this time."

"It's not that easy," Fredericks said. "They're not working any one time period. They move around a lot ... and that makes them hard to pinpoint. We've closed in on their operations three or four times already, only to discover they've just left when we got there. It's frustrating."

"What are we supposed to do now?" the colonel demanded. "Wait for them to kill us?"

"I doubt if they'll be back," Einar said. "Like we said, they move around a lot. They wrecked your camp to scare you off, and when you didn't go, they probably thought they'd do something else tonight. But now that you know they're here, they'll take off for another time-period again. No, you don't have anything to worry about. Just go about your business as usual."

"That's all you're going to do?" I demanded.

"That's all we *can* do," Fredericks said. "Unless you want to cancel the tour. But that's your business at this point."

"You ain't canceling the tour," the colonel said firmly. "We've scarce begun. And if them galoots come back well, I'm not afraid of a fight!"

"If they come back," Fredericks said firmly, "call us." Then he adjusted his Time Belt, flicked the switch, and he and Lieutenant Einar vanished.

After we told everyone what the Patrolmen had said, they weren't happy.

"What do you want us to do?" the colonel asked.

"Tomorrow afternoon, we'll pack up and move to a different time. The Jurassic period should be nice. There are quite a few interesting dinosaurs there, and I think a number of them would be suitable for a rodeo."

That seemed to satisfy everyone.

Dawn wasn't that far away, and nobody except Mallory seemed interested in sleep after that. After she retired, the rest of us sat around the campfire. We ate an early breakfast and talked about great rodeos. It seemed everyone had a different story to tell, and I could only envy them. My experiences with mind-tapes paled beside the real thing.

Dawn finally came, blushing the eastern sky with pastel reds and oranges and yellows. The sounds around us changed as nocturnal creatures—the insects, frogs, and small primitive mammals—all hid under plants or went underground. Meanwhile, the rest of the dinosaur world awoke. Birds cawed and flew overhead. Small duck-billed dinosaurs howled and moaned and blayed. Even the plant life perked up, leaves and flowers rising to meet the sun's rays.

And then, the Earth shook. Unpleasantly.

"What's that?" I stood and looked about. I saw nothing unusual, but my instincts told me something was wrong.

"Shush up there!" Joan Wesley Hardin commanded. She poised, listening. All the little dinosaur noises had stopped. "There!" she said, pointing. Distant treetops were toppling. Something *big* was headed our way.

Then, without warning, a triceratops burst into the clearing at the foot of our hill, between jungle and ravine. A solid sheet of bone extended over its neck and shoulders from the base of its skull. It brandished three horns (one short and on its nose, two longer and behind its eyes) like a prize bull. The creature was nearly as large as a full-grown elephant. Blood glistened on its scaly brown skin. Something had taken a bite from its hindquarters, but the wound hadn't slowed it down. Its flanks could take a lot of damage without causing it serious harm.

The thing knocking over trees in the jungle was getting closer. I felt the ground tremble faintly. Roaring again, the triceratops whirled to face the jungle. Its head lowered to charge.

"Watch this!" said Deadshot, taking aim.

"Awgrh!" I exclaimed—or something like that. I jumped in front of Deadshot. "What are you doing? You can't kill dinosaurs. You might change history!"

Deadshot grinned. "I just want a little target practice. Look at the barnacles on that sucker's head-gear. I betcha, oh, a night with Cleopatra that I can pick 'em all off without the little beastie noticing."

"Great idea, son!" said the colonel. He raised his six-shooter and drew a steady bead. "The left horn's mine!"

"Not if I get it first!" Joan snapped up her laser rifle.

"Now wait a minute!" I shouted. "The first person to take a shot is getting sent back to the present! You hear me?"

"Why?" Deadshot looked at me in confusion. "We're all expert shots. What could it hurt?"

"That's right!" the colonel blustered. "I say *whoa!*" His eyes widened and lit up like somebody had set a fire under him.

The others registered shock, fear, dismay, and horror. Deadshot went slack, so I took the laser from his hand. Then I turned around.

A Tyrannosaurus rex, between seven and eight meters tall, had emerged from the forest. Jaws gaping, it showed rows of razorlike teeth. Its tiny forearms twitched. When its black eyes focused on the triceratops, it let loose a horrible roar.

For the first time in many years, I knew fear. *This* was why I hadn't wanted to go back in time. It was like my Dad's death all over again. My muscles turned to jelly. I felt all cut up inside, and a lump the size of Texas rose in my throat. I couldn't think, could scarcely breathe.

"Roy," whispered the colonel, "what should we do?"

"Stay here," I managed to whisper back. "Don't attract their attention!"

The triceratops lunged, horns first. And I'll be darned if the tyrannosaur didn't twist just enough for the horns to miss. For a monster it moved like greased lightning. It sank its great fangs deep into the triceratops' back and began ripping and tearing with those deadly little claws.

The triceratops roared. It attempted to gouge its attacker but was unable to twist its neck far enough. Then it did the only thing it could do in its own defense: it slammed its twelve-ton body sideways, into the tyrannosaur, with all its might.

The tyrannosaur staggered backward, spitting out pieces of meat. Before it could recover, the triceratops gave it a gash across the belly. And I mean a deep one. Entrails showed.

The Tyrannosaurus rex, king of the thunder lizards, stood still for a moment. And then it began to sway. A river of blood poured from its stomach.

I'd have thought the triceratops would move in for the kill, but it didn't. That last chunk taken from its back had caused it more damage than I'd originally thought. Instead of delivering a fatal blow, it wavered. It was dizzy and weak, too.

The tyrannosaur gathered the last of its strength. It launched itself at the triceratops. The triceratops charged with a noise between a wheeze and a roar. Once more its horns penetrated deep into the tyrannosaur's belly. Then it reared back its head, lifting the tyrannosaur off the ground, completely impaling it.

"Hoo-whee!" said an awestruck Colonel. "I guess we're eating tyrannosaur steaks tonight!"

I don't know what we expected next … perhaps that the triceratops would finish off its foe, then limp off to heal or die. Instead, its legs buckled under the weight on its horns and both the varmints fell on their sides.

An incredible amount of blood poured from the triceratops' mouth and nose. It had been too weak to pick up the tyrannosaur, I realized. Its heart had burst from the strain. The tyrannosaur, meanwhile, gave a whimper and lay its head down.

All my feelings of revenge were gone by that point. The tyrannosaur had only been following its instincts. The only comfort I could take from the sight, now, was the knowledge that this scene had taken place eons before I had ever been born. Both the tyrannosaur and the triceratops had been fated to die this way. This scene was history.

Both dinosaurs lay there, faintly twitching, as the final sparks of energy in their bodies flickered and faded away.

"I can't stand seeing this," said Deadshot, snapping his fingers and holding out his hand. "Let me put the dumb critter out of his misery."

"Good idea," groaned Joan.

"I'm sorry," I said. "We've got to let it happen."

"Why?" exclaimed Deadshot. "It's going to happen anyway. There's no reason for it to suffer any more than it has to."

"That's just it," I said. "It has to." After ensuring the safety was kicked in, I tucked Deadshot's laser under my arm. "It happened this way before we were here, and now that we are here, we can't change it."

Suddenly I heard the *zzzzzt!* of a laser rifle firing. Everyone gasped, including me. Everyone but Joan Wesley Hardin.

The barrel of her laser rifle still glowed faintly from the shot she'd fired. She was scowling. Her expression was stern. But a single tear glistened on her cheek.

"Joan!" I exclaimed. "How could you do that?"

What she did, of course, was kill the tyrannosaur. The great dinosaur sprawled out with the unearthly stillness that only death can bring. Although I cannot say I was entirely unmoved by the sight, most of my emotions were submerged beneath the anger I felt.

"Don't you know if there are any significant ripples in the time stream, the Time Police can get a warrant and snuff you out of existence?" I shouted into her face.

She didn't even flinch. She looked at me so calmly that at first I thought she was making fun of me, or else was trying to make me angrier.

"He's right, girl," said the colonel worriedly. "I'm not sure even the extra fees the Texas Rodeo Association is paying can buy you out of this jam."

"Joan," said Alice. "This is weird. Not that I'm hoping this is what's happening, mind you, but it's strange to think that at this very moment the Time Police could be moving a day into the past beyond us, looking for you."

"It's highly unlikely," replied Joan, as matter-of-factly as if she had said the world was round.

"You never know," I said. "Big things have been known to result from tiny changes. Once our entire way of spelling the English language was changed because some poor goon stepped on a butterfly. The Time Police had to make a lot of permutations in the time stream to rearrange things back to normal. And you'd know that if you'd studied the history of time travel."

"What do we do now?" asked Alice. "Wait and see what happens?"

"Relax, folks," said Joan, stifling a yawn. She appeared pretty relaxed for someone whose existence might end at any moment. "Nothing's going to happen."

"How do you know?" I asked angrily.

"Because it's not my destiny to die here," she said. "I met one of my descendants. He said he had to meet me on account of my being such a legend in his time and all. He hasn't shown himself since. But now I know that I'm going to have children. That's how I figured if anybody could put the tyrannosaur out of his misery, it was me."

"The future is flexible, but the past is not," I told her. "You may have changed everything by killing the tyrannosaur. This descendant of yours may not exist now. When we return to the present, it could all be changed. If we don't exist there, we'll just wink out of existence like we'd never been."

"Do you think that happened?" she demanded.

"No. The chance is minuscule. But—"

"Then it was worth the risk," she said.

"I agree," said Ziggy. His tone implied he was right proud just to know her. "I would've done the same, if I'd thought of it first."

I glared at them all. "In case you've forgotten," I said, voice hard, hurting with every word. "*I* am in charge. When I tell you not to do something because it's too risky, I expect to be obeyed. *Instantly.* You've all just stepped over the line. Your tour is canceled."

Chapter Six

"**N**ow wait a minute here, son!" the colonel said. "You can't cancel because of a little thing like this!"

"I can," I said, "and I'm going to."

"See here." He took my elbow and pulled me away from the others. "Sure, Joan may have acted a bit too impulsively back there, but we couldn't just watch a dumb critter hurtin' like that. It cuts you up inside. You just *got* to help it."

"I understand how she felt," I said. "I wanted to do the same thing."

"There you go!"

"But I *didn't* do it," I continued, "because I knew better. I had already explained why we couldn't. She *knew*, and disobeyed my orders. That's a violation of the contract you signed before you took this tour."

"That's reading the letter of the law, not its intent," he protested.

"All time travelers have responsibilities, as the Time Patrolman at your indoctrination told you. Remember? And do you remember what he said about the dangers of changing history?"

He nodded, looking abashed.

I went on, "But it's more than that. Your cow-punchers have been going out of their way to flaunt my authority since we got here—like Deadshot's roping that drom our first day here. I may be young, but I know what I'm talking about!"

"You're correct," he said solemnly, looking down. "I see what you mean, and I'm sorry, Roy. But you have my word as a gentleman, if you give us another chance, you'll see a *real* difference."

I hesitated. "I'll make you a deal," I finally said.

"What's that?"

"We'll stay here. But I'm in on everything you do from now on. *And* you have to teach me to ride and rope droms."

"That's the spirit!" he said. "We'll make a cow-boy of you yet. Hey, everybody! We're staying!"

While the colonel explained our agreement to the others, I went to check on Mallory. I couldn't believe she wasn't awake, considering all the commotion from the dinosaur fight.

I stopped at her tent. "Mallory?" I called.

When she didn't answer, I called her name more loudly. Still no reply. Then I unzipped her tent's flap and peeked in.

She wasn't there. Her backpack was gone, and when I touched her sleeping bag, it was cold. She hadn't been here in some time.

I ran out, panicked. Where had she gone? Dinosaurs like the Tyrannosaurus rex were only one danger. There were poisonous plants and insects, swampy

bogs, and who knew what other traps for the care-
less explorer.

"Has anyone seen Mallory?" I called.

Everyone shrugged and looked around, as if
expecting to see her. Nobody had noticed her slip
away. *How long has she been gone?* I wondered.

Then I heard a rustling on the far side of camp.
I jogged over, the rest of the cow-punchers on my
heals. And there was Mallory coming out of the
jungle, leading our two escaped droms.

"What's wrong?" she demanded.

"We were worried about you," the colonel said.

"Didn't you hear me?" she asked. "When those
two dinos started ripping each other up, I went to
round up our droms."

Deadshot and Ziggy led the droms back toward
our corral.

I said, "I guess we were all too caught up to
notice."

"I guess," she said, smiling.

I noticed she didn't have her pack with her. I
felt certain I hadn't seen it in her tent, and when I
looked around camp, I didn't see it out there, either.
Perhaps I'm going crazy, I thought.

I let Wylde and Deadshot carve steaks from the
two dead dinosaurs, and we had a dinosaur barbecue
for lunch.

"I can't see why anyone would want to eat
this stuff," Mallory complained, nibbling on broiled
triceratops.

I had to agree. "It *is* a bit tough," I said. "But
perhaps some of the smaller dinosaurs are better."

She moved closer to me and sat down. "I've been meaning to have a talk with you," she said in that fake-friendly voice. "Do you think we might take a slight detour at some point?"

"Detour?" I asked slowly. "What do you mean?" This had to be what she'd been leading up to.

"There's supposed to be this comet, the one that wiped out all the dinosaurs."

I laughed. "But nobody knows when it came down. I wouldn't know what year to look, even if I wanted to. Which I don't. Too dangerous, thank you."

"Oh," she said, sounding like a disappointed child.

"Besides," I added, "it would probably take months, if not years, to pinpoint the exact day and time it came down. Our tour is only for three weeks."

"But what if I had the *exact* time the comet came down?"

"There's not much point in supposing that," I said. "You might as well assume it's coming down here, tomorrow!"

"I'm serious. If I knew, could we take a peek?"

I smiled, enjoying myself for the first time that day. "Sorry, Mallory. I'm more than busy enough already."

She stood, threw her plate and scraps into the disintegrator, and stomped off to her tent. Despite my best efforts, I think I smiled. I didn't like it when people tried to charm me into doing favors for them. Call it pride.

*   *   *

After lunch, we began packed up camp. I activated my Master Time Belt and shunted my tourists
from the Cretaceous period back to the late Jurassic.
This, I thought, *should put more than enough time
between us and any bootleg dinosaur-meat smugglers operating in the Cretaceous.*

I found myself squinting into a sun so bright it
hurt my eyes, set in a cloudless sky so blue it looked
unreal. Our hill had vanished, replaced by a grassy
plain. Far in the distance, dark shapes grazed ...
dinosaurs of some kind. The gully to the west had
been replaced by a sparkling blue lake. Tiny birdlike
creatures swam in the marshy spots close to shore.
To the south now stood a series of low, rocky hills.
A jagged bluff faced us.

"We'll set up camp over there," I said, pointing
to the hills. "We'll have no trouble finding high, flat
land."

Colonel Tom nodded. "Sounds good. The sooner
we get set up, the sooner we can get back to work."

I hefted my packs, and the others did the same.
Together, we lugged our equipment toward the hills.
Luckily we soon found a grassy little plateau. It was
the perfect spot, we all agreed.

Pitching tents and setting up electric barriers
to keep small varmints out didn't take long. In two
hours, we were done and ready to relax. Unfortunately, I didn't realize that relaxing for my tourists
meant finding more dinosaurs to rope or hogtie.

"Look there," said Deadshot, as we gazed down
on the lake. "What are those flying critters?"

Two large and rather peculiar-looking creatures were flying over the lake. Their feathers were a mottled mixture of blue and yellow, and they easily spanned between two and three meters from wingtip to wingtip. Their long beaks curved upward in front of their heads.

"Those are pterodaustros," I said. "They're a cousin of the pteranodon. They're probably looking for fish."

"Can I rope one of them pteros?" he asked.

I laughed. "Thanks for asking this time. Sure, go ahead. I don't think they'll be easy to catch, though."

Deadshot took careful note of the two pteros' flight patterns. They glided near one little spit of land each time they came around the lake. That looked like the most likely spot to rope them, I thought. He seemed to decide the same thing because, with a whoop, he grabbed a coil of rope and took off.

He reached the spit while the pteros were soaring over the far side of the late. Crouching down behind a small thicket of reeds, he made a lasso. Then he peeked out to watch the pteros circle back.

As they approached his hiding place, Deadshot stood, swinging his lasso. The first ptero either didn't notice or didn't care; perhaps it thought Deadshot couldn't reach it that high in the air.

"That thing's as stupid as a dodo," the colonel observed wryly. He'd come up beside me to watch.

"Wait and see," I said. "He doesn't have it yet."

Deadshot tossed his rope. It neatly looped over the first ptero's beak and slid down around its scrawny neck. For a second, the ptero flew as though nothing had happened. Then it came up short, wings beating furiously. Its beak opened wide, revealing rows of pointed teeth.

"Gwawk!" it shrieked.

Deadshot tried to reel it in. Only the ptero had no intention of coming down out of the sky. It darted first one way, then another. Deadshot nearly fell a couple of times, but always managed to catch himself in time. Finally he jammed his heels against a protruding rock and braced himself.

"Get 'im, boy!" the colonel hollered down. *"Yee-haw!"*

The pterodaustro tried desperately to escape. Deadshot began winding the rope around the rock. The creature strained at the end of the lasso, fluttering up and down like a kite caught in a gale.

"Got him!" he shouted back to us.

There couldn't have been much brain in the ptero's narrow head, but it was smart or it was mad enough to attack anything nearby. Whatever the reason, the pterodaustro wheeled around, glared at Deadshot, and dived straight toward him.

"Hey!" I shouted, pointing. "Behind you!"

Deadshot, laughing, didn't realize the danger. He was too pleased with himself, I guess, to wonder why the colonel and I were waving our arms and shouting. By the time he *did* realize something was up, it was almost too late.

The ptero swooped down, meaning to gouge him with its toothy beak. Deadshot hit dirt, and the birdlike reptile sailed over him. It sproinged to a stop when its rope ran out, and its claws grabbed at air as it fell to the ground.

At the same time, Deadshot picked himself up. He was plenty mad now.

"Toss me another rope!" he shouted to us. "I'll hogtie that buzzard!"

The colonel took a coil of polymer-plus rope from his belt and heaved it as far as he could. It fell twenty meters short. Deadshot ran, grabbed it, and started back with a look of grim determination on his face.

But the pterodaustro had other ideas. It waddled back to the rock and bit through the rope. Turning, it launched itself at Deadshot.

"Yee-ow!" Deadshot shouted. He threw the coil of rope, ducked, and rolled to the side. Unfortunately, he went the wrong way and tumbled into the lake with a terrific splash.

The pterodaustro's beak snapped on air. Nevertheless, it seemed satisfied. Cawing triumphantly, it flapped away. The lasso fell away from its neck as it came untied.

Everyone had by now gathered to see the excitement. Most laughed uproariously at Deadshot's predicament. When they finished, we all hurried down to the lake.

"I figure the problem here," Mallory said, as everyone pulled Deadshot to shore, "is that these dinosaurs simply aren't going to make good rodeo animals."

"I sure know what you mean," Deadshot said,

wringing out his shirt. "Give me a steer to wrestle any day!"

"We should go more toward the future," Mallory went on. "That way we could have the most evolved dinosaurs."

"I already told you," I said sharply. "I don't want to go looking for that comet, period."

"Whoa there, son," the colonel said. "Maybe she's got a good idea here. Least we can do is hear her out, right?"

I grumbled, but gave in. Perhaps I *was* letting my dislike for Mallory get in the way. We *were* here to set up a dinosaur rodeo. If she had a decent idea, though I hated to admit the possibility, perhaps I should look into it.

"I'm serious, Roy," she said. "Think about it. Why shouldn't we go after the most evolved dinosaurs—dinosaurs better suited for rodeo purposes?"

"Um," I said, thinking fast. Everyone was staring at me like I'd deliberately tried to sabotage the rodeo.

"Besides," she went on," the Jurassic is about as drab a time as you can find."

She had me there. Although we had dinosaurs aplenty in the Jurassic, we didn't have any flowering plants. They hadn't evolved yet. There were plenty of them in the Cretaceous, pretty much the same ones that grow wild in the age of humans.

But that still didn't make her argument valid.

"You're working on some wrong assumptions," I said. "The first is that the further you go into the future, the more evolved the dinosaurs get. Untrue.

Each period has its own unique set of dinosaurs. Changes in the environment, like the Earth warming or cooling, caused whole species of dinosaurs to die out. There are just as many rodeo-suited dinosaurs here. If you'll think back to the indoctrination lecture, you'll remember that that's why we're going to several time periods."

"But," Mallory began, then stopped.

Score one point for me. You can't argue with facts.

"Good thing we're paying *you* for the tour," the colonel said, giving me another bruising slap on the back. "Just keep on bein' the expert, son!"

Mallory didn't feel like going dinosaur-spotting with us that afternoon, so we left her to guard the camp. The rest of us packed up our binoculars, laser rifles (I gave a brief lecture on the importance of *not shooting anything*), and set off for the grasslands.

About an hour into our trek, we came to the edge of a dense forest. Winged reptiles flitted from branch to branch, and tiny ratlike mammals made *chit-chit-chit* noises at us. There were palm and cypress trees, as well as plenty more I couldn't quite identify. They didn't look much like their modern-day cousins.

"When are we gonna see some *real* dinosaurs?" the colonel wanted to know.

"Soon," I promised. "Come on!"

We hiked parallel to the forest. A few herds of small, chicken-sized dinosaurs hopped away, but we didn't see anything suitable for a rodeo. Still, I thought of the dark shapes grazing in the grasslands that morning, and I knew bigger dinosaurs were out there, somewhere. It was just a matter of finding them.

The land gradually became hilly again. The grass thinned.

I was just about to suggest we turn back when something suddenly crashed in the forest to our right. I jumped, startled, as something large and dark began to move.

"It's a brontosaurus!" the colonel announced, as a huge body slowly lumbered toward us.

"Apatosaurus!" I corrected him. "Brontosaurus" was an outdated term; the scientist who'd "discovered" the brontosaurus had accidentally pieced together bones from several different dinosaurs.

"I don't care *what* it is!" Colonel Tom bellowed. "Look at that thing!"

It emerged from the forest and stood blinking stupidly in the sunlight. This was an impressive specimen, twenty-five meters from snout to tail. Its tiny head was dull pink in color, turning into deeper red at the baggy folds of skin under its chin. Reddish-brown stripes alternated with black along its back. It slowly pushed into the open.

"If we could bring that sucker back up the line to the twenty-first century," the colonel exclaimed, "why the holo-movie and mind-tape stuntwork in the first year alone could earn enough credits to buy the Taj Mahal!"

"Is it safe?" Kansas Alice demanded.

"Sure," I told her. "It only eats plants, so it's not interested in us. Just don't let it step on you!"

The others seemed reluctant to get close. There was something daunting about a creature that huge. It dwarfed the tallest elephant.

The colonel finally screwed up his courage and moved toward the apatosaurus for a better look. We followed him.

But the seventy-ton dinosaur had ideas of its own. Turning, it waddled up a small hill and vanished over the top. I expected it to emerge on the other side, but it didn't.

"It's hidin' back there," Alice said as we moved closer. "It must know we're after it."

Colonel Tom signaled for us to wait, and began to climb toward the top of the rise. This one was his. I figured a look wouldn't hurt; the thing was too big to ride, and all of us together couldn't have hogtied it in a hundred million years. When he vanished over the top of the hill, the rest of us stood around grinning, just like kids.

Suddenly we heard a shout, followed by the hiss of falling rock and gravel, and a high, loud honking noise. The apatosaurus came thundering around the far side of the rise. Its serpentine neck doubled back to glance at the colonel, who was shouting desperately, and then it galloped into the forest.

We all ran up the rise. The colonel was still bellowing, so I knew there had to be trouble. Had it stepped on him?

I reached the top and paused in shock.

The colonel lay almost completely submerged in what at first appeared to be a swirled cone of mud. It was big enough to have filled a small storeroom. Then the breeze blew our way, and an unmistakable odor hit our nostrils.

"Eee-ooo!" Kansas Alice exhaled.

My mind raced with a thousand different explanations of what I was seeing, but only one made sense. Colonel Tom had fallen into a pile of apatosaurus dung. We all burst into laughter.

"Darn it," Colonel Tom said, "get me out of this!"

"Oh, no, Colonel," I said. "There's nothing in my contract about this. You got yourself in, so you can get yourself out."

Alice wrinkled her nose and said, "Colonel, just how did you get yourself into—into this mess?"

"I say, I was trying to climb the critter. The coast was clear, and then all of a sudden I was covered with this foul concoction!"

Luckily for Colonel Tom, his friends were willing to help.

"We'll have you out of there in two shakes of cow's tail," Ziggy said. He and Deadshot tossed the colonel a rope and hauled him out.

After that, he was ready to head back. He was taking it like a pretty good sport, I thought, even when everyone insisted on walking upwind of him.

Mallory had spent the day sulking. When we reported utter failure in finding any rodeo-quality dinosaurs, she didn't say, "I told you so," but she was thinking it, I could tell.

"You all had better excuse me," Colonel Tom said. "I do believe I'm going to change for dinner."

Everyone laughed, and it lightened the mood considerably. The colonel was good like that.

Later, when night fell, we sat around a glowing campfire. There's nothing like the smell of wood smoke on a warm summer night.

Mallory sat next to me. This time she had the nerve to slip her arm around my waist. I removed it as subtly as I could. More of her fake friendship, I thought; I wanted none of it.

"You know, son," the colonel said at last, "I've been thinking about the rest of the tour. What do you have in mind for the next leg of our little rodeo trip?"

"I considered the Triassic, but decided against it," I said. "The animals there are too primitive for what you want."

"Can't say this is what we want, either," Kansas Alice grumbled under her breath.

"Yeah," said Wylde slowly. "I liked the Cretaceous a good sight better."

"Any chance we can go back there?" Joan asked.

"One day isn't enough to judge the whole Jurassic," I said. "Tomorrow we'll have better luck."

The colonel, still smarting from his misadventure that afternoon, snorted angrily. "You'll do what we want, so long as we're paying for the privilege!"

I resented the colonel's imperious tone. "You signed a contract that said you'd do as your Time

Courier told you," I snapped back at him. "If that's not good enough, then we can head back to the twenty-first century right now!"

Before anyone could reply, a loud tearing noise shattered the quiet. I jumped, startled. The insects shut up; the night creatures paused. In the sudden quiet I heard thumping noises, like something heavy falling, from behind our tents.

Deadshot slowly stood, picking up his laser rifle. "I don't like the sound of this, Roy," he said.

"Everyone stand," I said softly. "Move slowly. Get behind the campfire. *Now.*"

They obeyed instantly. All of them had weapons out except Mallory. And she looked like she wanted one badly.

Then a full-grown allosaurus came charging out from between the colonel and Deadshot's tents. Its huge jaws gaped, revealing ferocious fangs.

It stared at us. We stared back. Though it was not nearly so large as a tyrannosaur, the allosaurus could kill a man with one swipe of its claws or one lash of its tail.

Suddenly it roared, showing a thin gray tongue and more sharp teeth than I cared to think about.

Deadshot aimed his laser rifle.

"No!" I said. I knocked the barrel down. "You can't kill dinosaurs!"

"It doesn't mind eating us!" Kansas Alice shot back.

The allosaur focused on her. It *charged!*

"Hey, big fella!" Ziggy shouted, dashing across the dinosaur's path. "Hey! Git up there!"

It tried to snatch him up in its jaws, but Ziggy rolled to safety. The brute hurtled past, growling, then skidded to a halt and launched itself at him again.

My tourists ran for the tents to get out of the way. I joined them, then looked back to see Ziggy roll out of the way again. He was still shouting, still taunting. He clapped his hands to keep the dinosaur's attention.

It charged again and again. Ziggy used all his rodeo clown skills to keep out of its way.

When it began to tire, puffing for breath, Ziggy danced in front of the campfire.

"Here!" he called. *Clap, clap!* "Come get me!" *Clap, clap!* "Hey there!"

It snapped its jaws. It clenched and unclenched its little clawed hands. Its sides heaved.

Ziggy danced forward, taunting, and that did it. The allosaurus rushed him again. At the last moment, Ziggy sprang to the side, tucking safely into a roll.

The allosaurus couldn't stop. Its momentum sent it straight at the fire. Its snapping jaws and demonic eyes were eerily lit from below, and then it stepped on burning coals.

It paused, stunned. I smelled sizzling flesh. Throwing back its massive head, it let out the most ear-splitting howl I've ever heard in my life. It did a strange, ponderous dance for a moment, shaking its paw. It gave another shriek of pain. Looking bewildered, holding the burnt foot like it was broken, it limped off on three legs. It gave an unearthly wail.

"Great job, Ziggy!" the colonel said. "I declare,

that was the greatest display of rodeo clowning I've ever seen!"

"Aw ..." said Ziggy, with all due modesty.

The others returned one by one, all clapping Ziggy on the back and telling him what a great guy he was. Me included. I was right proud to know him then.

Finally we sat in a circle again and listened to the allosaurus howling far away. The noise became increasingly faint with distance.

I felt sorry for the allosaurus, even it had intended to eat us. After all, it had only been following instincts.

"You know," Kansas Alice said, "I think this time period may have some decent critters after all!"

"You bet," I told her. "How'd you like to try to ride *him?*"

"I'll stick to shooting, thank you kindly!"

"If he had a muzzle ..." Joan mused. And Deadshot had a gleam in his eye, like he was seeing just that.

But then I noticed someone was missing. It was, of course Mallory.

Chapter Seven

"**U**h ..." I said. "Does anyone know where Mallory is?"

They all looked around.

"Tarnation!" The colonel leaped to his feet.

"I bet she ran into the grass to hide," Deadshot said. "I almost ran in there myself when you said I couldn't shoot the blamed thing."

"We'll have to look for her," I said uneasily. "She might have fallen in the dark and hurt herself. We'll start with the area around camp in teams, so nobody else gets hurt or lost."

The grass seemed like the best place to start, I thought. If she'd fallen and knocked herself out, we wouldn't be able to see her. I could imagine her lying in the dark, hurt, unable to move. We had to do something, and fast!

I fetched flash-lamps from our supply chest. By twisting the handle, you could let loose a flood of light, or narrow it down to a tight beam. Everyone took one, twisting them to full power. Our camp blazed to life.

"Remember what I said," I told them. "Stick

together in teams. Ziggy and Kansas Alice, Deadshot and Joan. I'll go with Wylde and Colonel Tom. We'll fan out behind the tents, go a hundred meters, and then come straight back. Keep an eye out for any trail she might have left."

"Right," the colonel said. "Let's jump to it!"

The colonel, Wylde, and I started forward, pushing through waist-high grass.

"Mallory!" I shouted. "Mallory, can you hear me?" The other teams did the same. Then we'd pause and listen for a moan, or a response of any kind. *Nothing.*

We searched for half an hour with no success. Finally I called everyone back. There were grim faces all around.

"We'll wait till morning, then start again," Deadshot said. "Right, Colonel? Roy?"

"I guess we'll have to," I said.

"We'd all better turn in, then," the colonel said. Then he looked at me. "Any chance we can turn up that electric whatsit that keeps them critters away? I'd rather not see another allosaurus tonight!"

"You got it." I went and turned up the current. We'd run a wire all the way around camp, and anything that brushed into it would get a mild electric shock. That hadn't been enough to stop the allosaurus, so I turned the switch to full power. *That* should keep anything out, I knew.

Then, as I turned to go to my tent too, the place in front of me rippled. Mallory appeared with

faint shimmer of light—she just popped into exis-
ence. Her hand was on her Time Belt.

"Mallory!" I shouted.

She looked at me, said, "Uh-oh," and started to
reach for her Time Belt again.

"Oh, no you don't!" I said, grabbing her wrist.
"Do you know how worried we all were?"

"I'm sorry," she said. "I just wanted to get away
from that *thing*."

I blinked. "And how did you get your Time Belt
to work on its own? I have an override . . ."

I pulled up my shirt and looked down. My override had been turned off. Quickly I snapped it back
into place. She must have done it when she'd slipped
her arm around my waist earlier that evening, I
thought, shocked.

"Roy," she said, "I'm sorry I did that. Honest, I
am."

"Get back to your tent," I told her. "We'll dis-
cuss this in the morning."

Hurt, head down, she walked back to her tent.
She went inside, then zipped it firmly shut. I snorted.
*Of course she wasn't lost. She's too contrary to get
herself lost.*

I'd have to think about this very carefully before
I did anything. It was one thing to lose a tourist to
a dinosaur. Those were the risks, and they came
with the job. My father had died because of them.
There was nothing you could do. It was quite another thing to lose a tourist through carelessness.
I'd almost lost her that way. It was, I told myself,
nearly as much my fault as hers. I'd *known* she'd

been trying to use me. Why hadn't I been more careful?

I had a feeling that, if I turned her in, I'd be laughed out of the Time Courier business. With a sigh, I decided to overlook it this time. But I *would* be on my guard from now on.

Quietly I went to each of our circle of tents, knocked, and told the inhabitant that Mallory had found her own way back. Yes, she was fine. No, don't get up she's gone to bed and you can see her in the morning. That seemed to satisfy everyone.

Then I went to bed myself, still grumbling.

I was up at dawn the next morning with all the dino-punchers—all except Mallory. This time I checked and found her snoring safety in her tent. One less thing to worry about, I thought, as I sipped hot coffee and stared out into space.

"Hey, Roy," Joan Wesley Hardin said. "There's a herd of duck-billed dinosaurs moving down toward the lake where Deadshot had it out with that crazy buzzard!"

"Oh, yeah?" I said, still distracted.

"Yeah, and Kansas Alice is planning to bulldog one."

That got my attention. I looked around and discovered the dino-punchers had cleaned up their breakfast trash and gotten started for the day. I hadn't even noticed.

With a sigh, I got up. "Sounds like fun," I told her. "Lead the way, Joan!"

We started down the hill together. It was another beautiful day, I noticed, with the sort of perfect, cloudless blue sky you only see in dreams.

I also noticed Joan looking at me funny. Giving a mental sigh, I realized something had to be bothering her. That was probably why she'd stayed in camp after the others left . . . she wanted to talk to me alone.

"Did you ever stop to think," she said, "that things might not be what they seem?"

"What do you mean?" I asked.

She frowned. "I don't know exactly, Roy boy, but there's something fishy about the way Mallory keeps disappearing."

"I don't get you."

She rolled her eyes, exasperated. "Let me put it to you this way. I've known Mallory for years. But for the last couple of weeks, since this whole dino-rodeo affair started, I can't say I've known her at all. Do you follow?"

"No."

Joan shook her head. "I'm trying to tell you the young lady has had something on her mind, something she's hasn't told anyone. It's clearly tearing her apart. Now do you get me?"

"A little better."

Come to think of it, Mallory *had* been disappearing an awful lot lately. Or not disappearing, but staying by herself. She often chose to remain at camp while the rest of us roped dinosaurs. I chewed on that for a while.

It took five minutes to hike down to the lake from our camp site. On the flat plain to our left I could see a herd of at least two hundred dinosaurs. These were camptosaurs, I thought, recognizing their blunt, almost ducklike bills. And they were big, at least seven meters long from nose to tail.

Several dozen of them were standing knee-deep in the lake, heads down, rummaging in the muck and mud. They looked almost comical. On the shore, females were tending their young. Males patrolled the outside of the herd, protecting them from any carnivores that might show up.

Colonel Tom and all the dino-punchers except Kansas Alice were sitting at the base of our hill, watching something very intently. I followed their gazes.

Kansas Alice was crouching behind a high screen of grass, giving herself enough rope to play out a lariat. She really *did* mean to lasso a camptosaur and wrestle it to the ground. Considering their size, I could only hope she had the sense to go after one of the young ones. Even that didn't seem like such a good idea, though. If a couple of adult camptosaurs went after her, she could be crushed under their three-toed feet.

She stepped out from behind cover and started swinging the lariat over her head. I saw that she was moving stealthily toward a pair of camptosaurs, a young one about half the size of a full grown bull and its mother. They were grazing. Their backs were toward Kansas Alice.

She raised her hand, gave a signal.

Wylde surged to his feet. "Hey!" he shouted. "Dinosaurs! Hey!"

As one, the dinosaurs all stopped. They raised their heads, listening, alert for danger.

Kansas Alice waited for the perfect target. When the young camptosaur raised its head, she let fly the lariat, and roped the little duckbill with consummate skill.

She must have expected the dinosaur to run, but it didn't. The entire herd shifted its attention to the forest behind them. They craned their necks, paying scant attention to Kansas Alice.

I had a notion something bad was about to happen.

From out of the forest bounded two ceratosaurs. One was slate gray and the other was sort of a dusty black. Each sported a single, gleaming horn from his snout. They looked almost like medieval woodcuts of dragons.

These ceratosaurs were not quite as big as the allosaur that had attacked us the night before. They were about the same size as the full grown camptosaurs. What they lacked in size they made up for in meanness and ugliness, though.

The camptosaurs bleated in terror. Mothers nudging youngsters closer together, and the herd seemed to condense as they closed ranks and started to move.

The two ceratosaurs were wise to this strategy, however, and split up. One circled for the right flank of the herd and the other circled for the left.

Kansas Alice hadn't even noticed the ceratosaurs yet. Roping the young duck-bill had taken all her attention. As the herd moved, the duck-bill began to drag her along.

"Yippee ki-yay!" she shouted, digging in her heels and pulling her hardest. She didn't know the black ceratosaur was coming up fast behind her. I guess she thought they were all bleating because she'd roped the young duckbill.

Then, from the way the ceratosaur suddenly changed course and headed straight for her, I realized he was no longer as interested in the herd as he was in Kansas Alice.

"Alice!" I shouted. Everyone else shouted warnings, too. It did no good. She either couldn't hear me or didn't want to.

Deadshot was the only one who'd brought a laser rifle. I grabbed it from his hand before he thought of using it, then ran for the herd. Halfway there I dropped the rifle and concentrated on speed. I figured I had a good shot at beating the ceratosaurs to Alice.

Those duck-bills were making a lot of noise, and they were now moving faster to escape the oncoming ceratosaurs. Their pounding feet began to raise a cloud of dust.

The roped youngster and his mother had been at the head of the pack. They weren't up to full speed and the others began to pass them. The mother seemed dimly aware that something was amiss, and she honked back at Kansas Alice in annoyance. She was either too preoccupied or too stupid to see the rope around junior's neck.

But Kansas Alice only took this as a sign of

success. I could see her grinning. She'd soon have the young duckbill bulldogged! She let out a western whoop that I could hear even above the noise of the herd. Of course she didn't see the ceratosaur closing in fast on the herd.

It was a toss-up whether I was going to reach her first, or whether she was going to end up as a snack for the ceratosaurs. Luckily the dust was so thick by now that you could hardly see. I lost her several times. The ceratosaur did, too, and that gave me the time I needed.

When I spotted her head bobbing just a few meters away. I tackled her. She released her lasso and we both rolled on the ground for a moment.

"Hey!" she cried. "What do you think you're doing?"

"I'm saving your silly life," I replied. The tails of both mother and baby camptosaur vanished into the dust cloud. The herd thundered around us.

Then Kansas Alice punched me in the stomach as hard as she could. Air wheezed from my lungs. I doubled over, trying to breathe. I couldn't explain why I had tackled her. I couldn't even speak.

That's when Kansas Alice screamed. She'd finally seen the monster stalking her. Its huge feet stopped moving when it heard her piercing cry. The dust was starting to clear as the herd moved farther and farther away.

I looked up at the ceratosaur through a drifting yellow cloud. Its jaws opened as it gathered itself for a leap.

My hand found its way to my Master Time Belt,

which was the reason I'd run down here. I had to be within twenty meters of Kansas Alice's Time Belt to be able to carry her through time with me. If Mallory could escape the allosaur by stepping into the future, we could escape the ceratosaur the same way.

I punched the settings, then tripped the switch.

Instantly the dust vanished. The ceratosaur disappeared. We were both lying on our backs, panting, with the sun beating down on us.

"Here they are!" Wylde suddenly shouted. He pushed through the grass and grinned. "Hey Colonel, they're alive!"

"Of course we're alive," I said, rising. "What happened to the ceratosaur?"

"It nosed around here for a few minutes, then galumphed off after the duck-bill herd," Wylde said. "We came down looking for you, but you were gone. What happened?"

"I shunted Alice and me fifteen minutes into the future," I said.

Then I helped Kansas Alice up. She murmured a brief word or two and started limping back toward camp.

"What was that?" I asked.

She turned around, her plug-ugly features grim. "I said, I'm sorry I hit you!"

We'd all had enough of dino-punching for the morning, so we headed back for camp. Colonel Tom walked beside me, and he seemed in an unusually good mood.

"I want to thank you for what you did," he said.

"No need," I told him. "That's my job."

"Sure there's a need," he said. "Alice ain't gonna say it, so someone better. It hurt her pride to have you bale her out like that, even if it did save her life. So thanks, son. I declare, if ever there's anything we can do for you, just let me know. You hear?"

I grinned and nodded. "Sure. Just don't any of you get yourselves killed, okay?"

"Fair enough, son, fair enough."

Mallory still wasn't up and about, so I checked her tent. I'd decided to keep a close watch on her for the rest of the tour, just to make sure she wasn't up to more trouble.

But trouble there was. Her tent was empty. And a very odd and very familiar set of tools lay out on top of her sleeping bag. My eyes widened in surprise.

A Benchley kit.

They were used by the Time Service to open the safety seals and work on a Time Belt's delicate innards. Where had she learned enough about Benchley Theory and Time Belts to open one up? And where had she gotten a Benchley kit? They were closely guarded by the Time Service. There never should have been a set in private hands.

And I would have sworn she hadn't had it with her when I'd checked the gear she'd packed. That meant what? That she'd gotten in back here, somewhere?

I frowned, remembering the dinosaur-meat smugglers. They'd strolled into camp that night like

they'd been expected. If Mallory had somehow con
tacted them ... or if she were *working* for them ...

I didn't know, and I didn't have enough facts to
guess. Right now, my options were pretty limited. I
could wait and hope she came back. Or I could call
the Time Patrol and tell them all about Mallory.

I had a pretty good idea where she'd gone.
She'd talked continually about the comet that struck
the Earth and wiped out the dinosaurs. And hadn't
she said hinted at something else? I frowned, wishing
I'd paid more attention to what she'd been babbling.
Hadn't she said something about ... if she knew
when the comet struck, would I take her?

I stepped into her tent and picked up the
Benchley kit. I'd need it for evidence. As I did, a
piece of paper fluttered out.

It was a date in the late Cretaceous, the *very*
late Cretaceous, and a time in the afternoon. Under-
neath, someone had written "Comet!!!" and under-
lined the word in red.

Well, I knew when she was, and I knew where
she was. The only thing I could do now was cancel
the tour, return my tourists to the present, and
inform the Time Patrol. They would either search
her out in the Cretaceous, go back in time and
prevent her from taking the tour to begin with ...
or wait for her to return to the present. When she
did get back, there would be several warrants out
for her arrest.

Of course, she'd be banned from ever going on
a time tour again, at the very least. If she did nothing
to change history, she might get off that easily. We

didn't need people like her messing up the past for the rest of us.

Grimly, I went to the colonel. "I'm afraid you're going to have to live up to our agreement," I told him.

"What?" he asked, surprised.

"Mallory is gone again." I showed him the Benchley kit, which he stared at blankly. "She used this to turn off the override in her Time Belt. Now she's taking a little trip on her own. She's probably looking for that comet."

"Whoa, there, son!" the colonel protested. "Just because *she* went off on her own doesn't mean you have to take it out on the rest of us!" And he started babbling about not getting their money's worth.

"Tell it to Time Tours," I said, heading back to camp. "You'll see them in an hour. Now start packing."

Chapter Eight

"**N**ow, son, let's not be hasty," Colonel Tom was at my elbow like a bothersome gnat. "We're not finished back here in the Jurassic!"

"If you think you should get money back, tell them at Customer Service. We had an agreement and I'm holding you to it."

I left the fuming Colonel and ducked into my tent. In a way, I was disappointed. I'd actually begun to enjoy the tour. Once I'd gotten over my hatred of dinosaurs, helping set up a dinosaur rodeo had been a fun idea. Leave it to Mallory to ruin everything.

Ziggy and Joan entered behind me.

"Don't try to talk me out of it," I said firmly, shaking my head and frowning. "I'm afraid there's nothing I can do. We have rules, you know."

"No," Joan said. "I don't think anybody can blame you. Not after the trouble we've all caused. Not just Mallory."

Ziggy nodded in agreement.

"Well ..." I softened a little. "You two haven't been any real trouble."

"It's very nice of you to say that, Roy boy," Ziggy said. "You're a good fellow."

"It's the truth." I continued packing my gear. "But that doesn't change anything."

"No, I suppose not," said Joan. "But isn't there anything *you* could do? Do we have to call in the Time Patrol? Look, I told you Mallory had been acting strangely. She's been *different*. Something's been bothering her. She really *doesn't* act this way normally."

"I'd hope not," I said.

Maybe if you could find her, you could talk some sense into her."

That idea hadn't occurred to me. I remembered the piece of paper in my pocket, the one with the date and time and the word "Comet" written down. I *knew* she was there. And I *didn't* like the idea of turning one of my tourists over to the Time Patrol because I hadn't been able to handle her.

It was tempting. If I canceled the tour, if I called in the Time Patrol to clean up the mess, it would be just like I'd failed as a Courier. If I brought her back on my own and kept the tour going, it really might be for the best. These people were supposed to be my responsibility, after all. I'd saved Kansas Alice's life that morning. Could I do any less for Mallory?

"All right," I finally said. "I'll give it a try. But if I can't find her, then the Time Patrol is going to have to deal with her. Okay?"

"Yes, sir!" Ziggy said. He seized my hand and pumped it up and down.

"Uh," said Joan, "you're not gonna get yourself in trouble by looking for her, are you?"

I shook my head. "It's against company policy, but Couriers are allowed to bend the rules a bit in emergency situations. I guess this qualifies as one. Besides, if it works, it'll save a load of grief and paperwork for everyone."

"You should tell the colonel," Ziggy said, still grinning. "He'll bust a gut thanking you!"

"We'll see," I said. I dumped the gear I'd already packed back on my bed, then followed them out.

While they went to tell Deadshot and Wylde, I headed for the colonel's tent. The flap was unzipped and I could hear Colonel Tom and Deadshot inside talking.

"Nobody's ever going to know the difference." Colonel Tom was saying.

"You're sure about that, Colonel?" Deadshot asked. "We won't get into any trouble, will we?"

"Just count on me, son," the colonel said.

I didn't like the sound of that. What were they up to? There was no way of telling from where I stood. It looked like I'd have to confront the problem head-on.

Rather than burst in on them, I sat down to wait. Soon they lugged the colonel's two packs out of the tent.

When the colonel saw me sitting there watching him work, he got an angry look on his face. "Don't think I'm gonna take this lying down, son!" he said. "I've got friends in the Time Service. *Power-*

ful friends. They aren't gonna be happy, with you canceling my tour!"

"I'm sure," I said dryly.

"I paid extra, *plenty* extra for special treatment, and special services. When they hear about how you've treated us, you'll be lucky if they'll let you clean the Time Service parking lots!"

"Maybe they won't be as upset as you think." I pointed to his gear. "Let's see what you've got in there."

The color drained out of Colonel Tom's face. He hadn't been expecting me to fight back.

"What do you mean?" he said.

"Article seventeen of the Time Tours contract, which you signed, has a clause that gives the Time Courier 'the right to search all personal effects for illegal contraband before returning to the twenty-first century.' So let's see what you've got in those bags, Colonel."

Deadshot looked positively sick, but the colonel was doing his best to act like nothing was out of line. "See here, do you mean to tell me that you think I'm trying to do something illegal? That's slander, son. You could be sued for defamation of character. Why, I—"

"Save it for later. Open 'em up. Let's see what you've got in there!"

Colonel Tom made no move to open his bags, so I stepped forward, prepared to do it myself if I had to.

I saw something glint in Colonel Tom's hand.

e was holding a Bowie knife in a very threatening
ay.

"Where I come from," he said menacingly, "pri-
ate property is private property."

"So you've got a knife, have you?" I said, trying
ot to sound scared. "Well, so have I."

I slipped my jackknife out of my back pocket
nd opened it up. The blade was less than half the
ngth of the colonel's Bowie knife, but it was the
est I could do.

"Are you threatening me?" the colonel bellowed.
Are you threatening *me?*"

"Not at all," I said, smiling amiably. "I just
ought you wanted to compare knives. Yours is
igger than mine, but I keep my blade pretty sharp."

The colonel clearly didn't know what to do. I
ad called his bluff and he knew it. From all I'd
en, the colonel was a kind and gentle soul, and
e indignant act just didn't sit right with him.

All the others had come running at the first
unds of argument. Now Deadshot reached out and
ut a hand on the colonel's wrist. "Better put that
way," he said.

The colonel stared at me for a moment, but
nally did as Deadshot told him, sheathing the Bowie
nife in a rawhide scabbard. "Ain't nothing much,"
e said. "Just a few old dinosaur teeth and bones."

"You know there's a law against bringing those
ack to our time," I said.

"It's a stupid law."

"That doesn't mean we don't have to obey it."

"Well, them varmints was dead anyhow," Colo-

nel Tom blustered, as he pulled a few sun-whitene
bones out of a bag. "I didn't figure there was an
harm in it."

"There might not be, but if there is, it's a whol
lot more serious than just a few smuggled bones.
you want dinosaur bones, you'll have to settle fo
the hundred-million-year-old variety instead of fres
specimens. What happened, did some collectors hea
you were going back to the age of the dinosau
and ask you to bring a few samples back? For
handsome price?"

The colonel looked mortified. "Never!" he sai
"They're for my dog, Rex!"

"Rex?"

"That's right, the purtiest morgrel you ever di
see!"

"Don't get him started about Rex," Joan sai
rolling her eyes. "He'll spend hours talking abou
that mutt if you let him!"

Colonel Tom finished dumping out the bone
"You ain't gonna turn me in, are you, son?"

I thought about it for a few seconds. "No,
don't think so, Colonel. Just don't try to smugg
anything else back."

He brightened. "Well, that's mighty straight
you."

"And the reason I was waiting out here," I wen
on, "was to tell you we weren't going back. At leas
not right away. I'm going to find Mallory first."

They both looked grateful.

"Since everyone is here," I said, "I might as we
get started now. This is the plan, so gather around

They did so, listening eagerly. "I'm going to try to find Mallory. Hopefully she'll be standing there waiting to see the comet. If she is, I'll just grab her and bring her back. I'll set my controls to return just a few minutes after I leave, so you won't be kept wondering long. However, in case anything *does* go wrong, I want you to be able to return to the present and tell the Time Patrol what happened. So I'm going to turn off my Master Time Belt's override switch. This *is* a violation of company policy, so I want you all to promise you won't abuse the privilege."

Everyone promised right away, so I switched off the override. Their belts were now active. Theoretically, they could now travel to any moment in the past.

"Just get Mallory back," Joan said.

"I think you better take a laser rifle," Deadshot said. He handed me his. "Just in case."

"Thanks," I told him.

Then I set my Master Time Belt for the day and time specified in Mallory's note, handed the note to the colonel for safe-keeping, and shunted.

Trees appeared around me. I was in a little grove of cottonwood trees, and gently rolling hills surrounded me. There were flowers everywhere; they gave the air a scent like rich perfume. Slowly I turned, looking for any sign of Mallory.

On the other side of the grove, I found a human footprint. The boot was smaller than mine; it had to be Mallory's.

I started off in the direction her footprint indi-

cated. As I walked, I tried to figure out where I'd b
heading if I were Mallory. The crater from the come
had been found in recent years, right in this area
but she could be anywhere. After all, she wouldn'
be standing in the path of the comet when it cam
down, would she?

Impatient and angry, I scuffed at the groun
with my boots. I had to find her and get her out o
the late Cretaceous, I kept telling myself. It was a
matter of pride.

Then I heard a woman scream.

Chapter Nine

"**M**allory!" I cried.

Not two hundred meters to the south, I saw a pack of snarling deinonychuses in hot pursuit of a woman. These dinosaurs weren't much larger than a human, except for their two-meter-long tails. They made up for their relatively small size with their speed and ferocity. Rapidly they closed the gap on their prey.

Instantly, I unshouldered the laser rifle and fired. The laser beam struck the ground a few centimeters in front of the pack's leader. The deinonychus didn't even slow down.

I fired again, this time closer. Dry grass burst into flame right in front of the leader's face, then died. The sudden fire and puff of smoke brought the startled deinonychus up short. It hissed. The rest of the pack milled around in confusion.

The woman kept running, gaining a few meters. Then the deinonychus took up the chase again.

I fired my laser rifle again, sweeping the beam in a broad arc, starting a long brush-fire between

the woman and the dinosaurs. Flames climbed hig
in seconds. The dinosaurs turned and fled.

The brushfire died out when it hit a rocky are
I scarcely noticed; I was looking for Mallory. She'
run into a cottonwood grove, this one larger an
darker than the one where I'd originally appeared.
caught a flash of sun on metal, then lost sight of he
among the trees.

"Idiot," I muttered to myself. Had I expecte
her to be grateful?

I shouldered my laser rifle and gave chase. Soo
I was pushing my way into the shady knot of wood

"Mallory!" I called out, looking from one sid
to the other. "Mallory, it's all right. I've got a lase
rifle with me."

I paused to listen, but didn't hear anything. Wa
she ignoring me? Or had she used her Time Belt t
escape? I shook my head. *If she did, I'll never catch
her!*

As I came around a huge moss-covered log
though, a foot seemed to come out of nowhere. I
caught me square in the Time Belt.

"Huh!" I groaned, doubling over and dropping
the laser rifle. A small figure scrambled out from
behind the log, grabbed the rifle, and pointed it a
me.

"Mallory," I moaned, "what are you doing?"

I looked up at her, and it was only then that
realized she wasn't Mallory. This woman resemble
her, but her hair was a shade darker than Mallory's
and she was a little shorter.

"Stay right there, mister," she said. She kept the laser rifle pointed at my chest.

"I just saved your life, in case you've forgotten."

"I haven't," she said. "But that doesn't make you a friend. How do you know my sister? Are you with the Time Patrol?"

"No, I'm a Courier." I hoped my Time Belt was still in good working order. "You're Mallory's sister?"

"That's right, I'm Linda Byrne," she said.

"I'm Roy Jones. Pleased to meet you, Linda." I took a step toward her and extended my hand.

"Hold it," she warned. "I still don't trust you."

"What do you think I'm going to do? Steal the silverware?"

She smiled a little. "A woman can't be too careful," she said, lowering the laser rifle's barrel a bit.

"I agree. Look, I don't know what you're doing here and I don't care. I've come to find Mallory. She tampered with her Time Belt and took off. I tracked her here. If she's willing to come back peacefully and cooperate for the rest of our tour, I'll look the other way. If not, then I'm going to turn the problem over to the Time Patrol."

"I'm afraid I can't help you."

"You're just making things harder on Mallory."

"It's not that I *won't* help. I *can't.* You see, Roy, I haven't got the faintest idea where Mallory is. I didn't even know she was here till you told me."

"Then maybe," I said slowly, "you'd better tell me what's going on."

"That's a tale and a half." She laughed, relaxing

a bit more. She was pretty when she smiled, muc
like her sister.

"Can I have the laser back?" I said. "It belong
to the Time Service, and they get upset when I don
return stuff."

"Maybe later. First, I'll tell you how and why I'
here, and then you tell me about my baby sister

I sat and folded my arms. "I'm all ears."

"Well, our Mom was a paleontologist, and onc
time travel to the Mesozoic became possible, Mo
tried to pinpoint the date of the comet's impac
Using carbon-dating, she worked it out to within
few thousand years. She was going to explore th
time period and take holo-camera pictures to prov
she was right."

"And she was wrong?" I asked.

"She got close, but never finished. Mom die
too young."

"I'm sorry," I muttered.

"That's okay." Linda seemed to appreciate m
sympathy, at least. "It was up to me to carry on fc
her. Then I met a man who said he could bring m
back here."

"A Time Courier?"

"He used to be one, before he went renegade.'

I'd heard of renegades. Stolen Time Belts gav
them the means to plunder history. They smuggle
ancient artifacts, gambled on horse-races and spor
ing events whose outcomes they already knew, stol
valuable art treasures, and generally made life toug
for the Time Patrol. They were doubtless the sam
people who butchered dinosaurs and carried boo

leg meat to the twenty-first century. Renegades were pretty desperate characters. No wonder Linda had been worried about the Time Patrol!

"Where are your partners in crime now?" I asked.

"Looking for me, I imagine."

"Then you're lost?"

She frowned, and for a moment looked close to tears. "No, I'm not lost. They wanted me to help them. Some of the things they're doing here are really horrible. I couldn't butcher dinosaurs! I told them that. They don't trust me now. I heard them talking about it ... so I ran away."

"So you're avoiding both the Time Patrol and the renegades. You've got yourself into a fine mess, Linda."

"I know. But what can I *do?*"

"Start by trusting me. I'll help you if I can."

She sighed and handed the laser rifle back to me. "I guess I have to trust you," she said.

I accepted the laser. "If I was with the Time Patrol, you'd already know it. And I guess you know I'm not a renegade."

"I can't believe that dumb kid actually came after me," Linda said, sounding both frustrated and pleased with Mallory's actions. "That's—"

A muted *bang!* sounded behind me. Damp bark and moss flew in all directions. Somebody was shooting a projectile gun!

I grabbed Linda's hand and started running. More gunshots rattled around us. After a few minutes the shots grew more infrequent. At last, when I couldn't hear any more gunfire, I pulled Linda under the roots of an immense old banyan tree. It was sort of like a cave in there.

"Your renegade friends, I assume," I whispered. "I think we lost them."

"Not quite." It was a man's voice, gravelly and deep. I peered around the gnarled root to my left, and there were three of the toughest looking hombres I've ever laid eyes on. One had an eyepatch over his right eye. He seemed to be the leader. The second was a centimeter or two shorter, blond, with a huge scar across his left cheek. The third was smaller and darker. His lip curled back in a sneer. All three held pistols, and all three pistols were pointed at me.

"Put down that laser rifle," said the one-eyed man.

This isn't my day, I thought. Slowly, I did as instructed. The short renegade picked up my laser rifle.

"Linda, honey," said the one-eyed man, "why don't you introduce us to your friend?"

"You tried to kill us," Linda said.

"Now, you know that's not true. We were just trying to show you we mean business. Come on out here. Both of you."

We crawled out. The big man smiled and nodded like he was meeting me at a church social. "Still didn't catch the name."

"Roy," I said. "Roy Anikulapo Jones."

"Well, pleased to meet you, Roy. I'm 'Time Runner' Thompson. You can call me T.R. My boys are Joe and Lars."

Joe and Lars grinned. Neither of them had a full set of teeth.

"Start walking," Lars said in a heavy Scandinavian accent. It sounded like *Start valking.* So Linda and I walked, our three captors behind us.

"You're a Time Courier, huh, kid?" T.R. Thompson asked.

"That's right."

"Where are your tourists?"

"I sent them back to the present to get the Time Patrol."

T.R. snorted. "Sure you did."

I glared at him. "One of my tourists snuck off to see the comet that killed the dinosaurs. I thought it would be easier to get her myself. Kinder, too."

"Oh, you're a real humanitarian!" T.R. seemed to be enjoying himself at my expense.

I shut up. I'd told them more than I should have already. At least, when I didn't show up in the Jurassic, my tourists would be able to tell the Time Patrol what had happened.

"Where are you taking us?" I asked, to change the subject.

"Oh, you'll see," Thompson said. "It'll be a nice surprise for you, Roy."

He brought us out the other side of the cottonwood grove, back the way Linda had come. Finally we reached to a scrub-covered hill. Lars and Joe moved some brush, revealing a cave.

"Go in," Thompson said, giving me a shove in the back.

I did. The cave opened up into a huge chamber. The air inside smelled sweet, too sweet, like somebody had left meat lying in the sun too long.

And standing there pretty as you please, hands on her hips, was Mallory.

Chapter Ten

"**R**oy!" Mallory exclaimed. "What are you doing here?"

"I should ask you the same thing," I said. I noticed her hands weren't tied. T.R. hadn't forced her to stay here. She'd come of her own free will.

I glanced over at Linda and found a lot of different emotions playing across her face. Confusion was the biggest.

"Mallory," she said at last, "thank goodness you're all right. Roy really had me worried!" The sisters hugged briefly.

T.R. watched them, smirking the whole while. "A very touching family reunion, I'm sure," he said. "First, let's see the ransom."

"Ransom?" Linda and I asked at the same time.

"Sure," Mallory said. Now it was her turn to look confused. "I got a note saying they'd kidnapped you, Linda. Didn't you think I'd save you?"

Suddenly things started making a whole lot more sense.

"I wasn't kidnapped," Linda said, then she began explaining how she'd hired T.R. and his friends to take her back to see the comet their mother had been looking for.

T.R. abruptly cut them off. "You'll have enough time for that later!"

I asked, "It was Lars and Joe I saw in our camp that night, wasn't it?"

"That's right," T.R. said. "I sent them in to get the money. After we had it, we were supposed to release Linda here. Unfortunately, you scared them off. We watched the camp until the Time Patrol showed up, then took off. Too hot for us there!"

"The next day," Mallory said, "Joe snuck into camp while I was guarding it alone. He gave me instructions on how to get here, and showed me how to fix my Time Belt."

"But what about the comet?" I asked her. "I thought that's what you were after."

"It *was*," T.R. said. "Until your Courier friend showed up." He rubbed his jaw. "He complicates things. I'm going to have to think about this some. Meantime, I don't want you going anywhere. Lars, get their Time Belts."

Mallory removed hers and handed it over. While all eyes were on her, I let my right hand inch toward my controls. If I could shunt, I'd be back with the Time Patrol before they knew what hit them.

"Uh-uh," T.R. said, suddenly nudging me with the barrel of my own laser rifle. "Easy there, kid. Keep your hands safe."

Then it was my turn, and I had to surrender my Master Time Belt. As I did so, a cold, sick feeling welled up inside me. Things couldn't get much worse. T.R. took both belts (it seemed Linda wasn't wearing one) and locked them in a storage chest. He kept the key on a ring on his belt.

"Now," T.R. said, "I don't want you three getting bored. I have a little bit of work for you. If you do it well, maybe we'll feed you dinner."

"What are you talking about?" I said.

"In there. Next room." He nudged me again with the barrel of my laser rifle. I knew better than to resist, and so I headed with Mallory and Linda toward the back of the cavern.

The sickly-sweet smell got stronger. Then we passed through a door-sized hole into a chamber that served as a slaughterhouse.

There were cut-up dinosaurs everywhere. The processed meat had been preserved in a portable stasis field that hummed softly in the far corner. Batteries were piled high beside it; I guess it took a lot of power. Anything you put in a stasis field goes into a state of suspended animation until you take it out: very smart of them to use it to preserve dinosaur meat, I thought.

"Yep, we're in the dino-burger business," T.R. said gleefully. "Quite a call for 'em sixty-five million years in the future ... for those chefs who can afford them."

"I can't believe you'd slaughter dinosaurs this way!" I said. "It's ... it's horrible!"

"Not horrible, Roy. *Brilliant.* This is the most profitable scam a time traveler can run. The Time Patrol never comes this close to the comet."

I turned to T.R. "But you can't just go aroun
killing dinosaurs indiscriminately."

"Indiscriminately? We wouldn't think of it, Roy
Remember, this is the tail end of the dinosaur age
They're all going to die anyway."

I shook my head. "But after they die, scavenger
will need them for food. Dinosaurs can't feed human
alone!"

He smiled. "There's the beauty of it. We onl
take the best cuts of meat. There's plenty left fo
scavengers. If they don't get enough from one body
they can always eat another."

"But what about something happening to alte
history permanently?"

"I'm not stupid, Roy. I periodically travel to th
nineteenth century. If there's ever anything wrong—
and there hasn't been yet—then we just go bac
and stop ourselves from killing any dinos that day
Besides, we really *don't* want to mess up the time
line. If we did, we'd lose all our customers."

"There's a certain twisted logic there," I had t
admit.

He grinned.

"What are you going to do with us?" I asked.

"Ever dress out a drom?"

"Yuck!" Linda showed such revulsion that I seri
ously wondered for a moment if such a suggestio
had made her run off in the first place.

"Honey, you and I are going to have a littl
talk," T.R. said. He grabbed her by the wrist and
dragged her off toward the back of the cavern. Lind
struggled, but T.R. was too strong for her. I lunge

at him, but he knocked me flat with a backhand. He was far too strong for me, too.

"Drop 'em, boys!"

There were three audible clanks as weapons hit the cave floor. When I could see straight again, those three desperadoes were holding their hands high in the air. Mallory let out a delighted whoop. Propping myself onto my elbows, I peered back at the doorway and saw a familiar figure.

"Ziggy!" I shouted.

The Jamaican cowboy had his laser pistol pointed at T.R. and his cohorts. The renegades didn't look happy.

"I thought I'd better follow you," Ziggy said. "Good thing I did, too."

"It sure is," I agreed.

Mallory and Linda both armed themselves with the pistols and laser rifle our prisoners had dropped. I went back and frisked all three of them, coming up with two more sidearms and three nasty looking knives. I also took T.R.'s ring of keys.

Noticing a suspicious lump in Lars' boot, I made him turn over a switchblade he had hidden there. Then I backed away with all their weapons in my arms.

"They've got elephant guns and explosives in that chest over there," Linda said, pointing. "And they have more guns in the front room."

"Do you know where they keep rope?" Ziggy asked her.

I said, "We don't need rope."

"The stasis field," Mallory said.

"Good idea," Ziggy said, giggling a bit. "Pack 'em in with their dino-burgers!"

"Hey," T.R. said. "You can't put us in that!"

"Oh, no?" I said. "I'm sure it's better than what you intended to do with us."

"It's inhuman!"

Ziggy grinned wickedly. "In you go, boys."

The three thugs walked over to the field generator with a helpless shrug.

"At least it's fast," T.R. said.

With that, he plunged into the stasis field. He stopped moving, a curious smile locked on his face. He might have been frozen solid. He effectively was—every atom in his body had stopped moving. Joe growled and followed his boss, then Lars. They looked like three ugly statues in there.

"Well, we're rid of them," Mallory said.

I walked over to her. She lowered her weapon and gave me a hug. "You came after me, you idiot," she said. "Don't tell me you did it because it's your duty, because I won't believe you. You should have called in the Time Patrol."

"You're right, I *should* have," I said. "You can thank Joan and Ziggy. I came after you because they asked me to . . . because they care what happens to you. I respect that."

She gave Ziggy a hug, too, and I gave him a clap on the back and a hearty handshake. We all thanked him for saving us.

"Well, shucks," he said, blushing. "Glad to help. Only what are we supposed to do now?"

"I guess we had better notify the Time Patrol," I said.

"No way," Mallory said. "We came here to get evidence of the comet, and we're not leaving without it."

Linda said, "According to our research, *this* is the big day. It won't take long. We'll leave right after it, I promise."

It seemed Linda had a holo-camera with her, along with tapes and all the other equipment they'd need. They were both experienced at camera-work. That made sense; Mallory had been a reporter, after all."

"We don't have much time," Mallory said. "We'd better get started. Where's your stuff?"

Linda said, "I hid it in another cave. T.R. had quite a temper and might have destroyed it."

"Well, I hope it's still in one piece," she said. "Where's the cave?"

"Not far. All we have to do is retrace my steps. We should be able to find it."

I said, "Let's hurry. I don't like leaving them here."

After we retrieved our Time Belts from the chest in the first cavern, we walked back toward the place I'd shot at the deinonychuses. Before we got there, however, I saw thick smoke ahead. Something was burning.

"Oh, no!" I said. "The brushfire I started didn't go out after all!"

"That's okay," Linda said. "The fires the comet

starts are going to make yours look like a garden barbecue. There it is!"

For a moment I thought she meant the comet. I actually looked up at the sky. But she was pointing to a series of low cliffs in the distance.

Half an hour later, as we drew closer to the cliffs, Linda pointed out a rope hanging down from a cleft in the bare rock.

"That's where I rapelled down," she said. "They started shooting when I got halfway down. I couldn't move very fast lugging the holo-camera, so I ditched it in that cave at the bottom."

It didn't turn out to be much of a cave, but the holo-camera and accessories were safe inside, sealed in airtight bags.

"All we have to do is set it up near the impact site," I said.

"We're almost close enough right here," Linda said. "But we'll have to be on the other side of these cliffs for the best view."

I looked at the rope she'd used. "Do we climb there?"

"No, we can take the pass." She pointed. "I used the rope because I was in a hurry."

"We've got all the time in the world now." I grinned and patted my Master Time Belt. "If the comet strikes before we get to the other side, we'll just shunt a few hours into the past and start over again."

It didn't take long to get through the pass. It was steep, but not too difficult. On the other side, the ground sloped to a plain that would look a lot different in the twenty-first century. In fact, I reminded myself, tomorrow it would be one vast crater.

We stopped at a place where the ground was level. Two huge boulders kept us out of sight of the larger dinosaurs. Ziggy and I peered around them.

A herd of ten-meter-long hadrosaurs grazed patiently in the distance, and occasionally a pterosaur's wings broke the sky. We could smell salty air from the inland sea on the horizon. Doubtless it teemed with mosasaurs, ichthyosaurs, and all sorts of other prehistoric fish.

I admit I was excited. To think I was actually going to see the great comet hit!

Linda and Mallory worked quickly on their holo-camera. It stood on a little tripod, its three lenses pointed at the comet's future impact site. In a few minutes they were done. Now we had nothing to do but wait for the show to start.

Then I heard the sharp *crack!* of a gunshot. A bullet struck sparks from the rock next to me, and shards of stone peppered my hands and face.

I whirled to see T.R., Lars, and Joe standing in the pass behind us. T.R. held a smoking elephant gun.

Chapter Eleven

"**N**ot again!" I cried.

"Nobody move," T.R. said in a mocking tone. "You might get hurt."

We didn't need to be told to drop the guns, knives, and laser rifle. Joe collected them, while Lars pushed us up against the large rocks and searched us for hidden weapons. When he found his switch-blade, he took it back with a happy sigh. Then he took our Time Belts.

Chortling, Lars backed away. "They're clean, T.R.," he said.

Linda asked the obvious question: "How did you get out of the stasis field?"

"We were going to recharge the field's batteries today," T.R. said. "I figured there were only about three or four hours of full-power left when we walked into it. When the field finally began to weaken, it was like walking through molasses. It took forever, but we made it out. Lucky for us, huh?"

I recalled T.R.'s devil-may-care attitude when he entered the stasis field. At the time I had chalked it up to reckless bravado. I'd know better the next time I had to deal with him ... if there *was* a next time.

"So what now?" I asked.

"What now? We've got a job for you back at the cave," he said amiably. "We figure on spending another two weeks in this time period. You can help us until then. If you're good boys and girls, we'll even take you to our next camp, too. There are all sorts of jobs you'd be perfect for."

"Oh," Mallory said, sounding relieved.

"What did you think we were going to do, stake you out on an anthill?" T.R. demanded. "We may be renegades, but that doesn't mean we're killers."

By his rights, I suppose he was being quite reasonable. But I had no intention of spending the rest of my life as a slave in the last days of the Mesozoic. Besides, if Linda's calculations were correct, there weren't going to *be* any more last days of the Mesozoic. This was it, any minute now.

I looked up at the sky. Sweat was trickling down my back and sides. How much time did we have left? Hours? Minutes? Seconds? If something went wrong, at least we would have been able to escape before. Now, without our Time Belts, we'd be sitting ducks if the comet hit.

"What's the holo-camera for?" Lars asked.

"We were just setting it up," Mallory lied. "I'm a reporter. I was going to break the bootleg dino-meat smuggling story, and we needed a few background shots."

T.R. looked through the holo-camera's viewer.

"Well, look at that!" he said. "Looks like an alamo-saurus. Wait, there's more than one!"

I didn't need to look through the multiple lens arrangement to see what he was talking about. A herd of enormous, long necked dinosaurs was ranging across the distant plain. Rearing up on their stubby hind legs, they cropped the leaves from the tops of trees. I found something very peaceful and charming about the ungainly creatures.

"Lars," T.R. said, "look after our friends while Joe and I go down to pick off a few of those alamos."

"What if they give me trouble?" he asked.

"Hurt them," T.R. said. "But keep them healthy enough to work. Right?"

"Right, boss," Lars said, grinning.

Then T.R. and Joe set off, carrying their elephant guns. I couldn't believe they were so happy about slaughtering such peaceful creatures as alamosaurs.

"What scum," Mallory whispered. There was nothing we could do, not with Lars holding that elephant gun on us. In my mind, I ran through desperate plan after desperate plan. There weren't any easy solutions.

But perhaps, if Lars were as dumb as he looked . . .

"Lars," I said suddenly, "you know what they named those dinosaurs after?"

"Uh-uh." Lars didn't think a whole lot, period, it seemed.

"Remember the, oh . . . what was it?"

He looked at me strangely. "Alamo?" he said.

Just as he said the word, I let out a Texas war

whoop that would have shaken the leaves off the trees. Then I leaped at Lars, and Ziggy was right on my heels.

Lars didn't flinch. When I tried to punch him, he deflected the blow easily, then spun me around. Ziggy ran smack dab into my chest, and we both collapsed in a heap at Lars's feet.

Lars stuck the cold gun barrel under my chin. "Don't do that again," he said.

"We wouldn't dream of it," I replied.

"Sit down over there," he said, pointing to the rock. "Where I can keep an eye on you."

Luckily T.R. had made it clear he wanted us alive. Or maybe Lars had done all the meat-chopping up till now, and was looking forward to having a replacement. Whatever, he was keeping a closer watch on us for the moment.

As we sat and waited, the silence burred in our ears. At last we heard an echoing rifle shot ... the first of the alamosaurs had fallen.

"We've got to do something," Mallory whispered to me. "They're going to slaughter those poor dinosaurs!"

"Right now, we'd better concentrate on staying alive," I told her. "Remember what's coming down?"

"He's right, you know," Lars said. "With all that extra work coming, you'd better rest." He rubbed the barrel of his rifle like he wanted to use it.

The shooting continued. At least we couldn't see the slaughter from where Lars had made us sit. The dinosaurs began honking pitifully. I felt sick listening to them.

Lars was loving every minute of it, though. He stood and began to shout encouragement to his partners. Never mind that they couldn't hear him this far away.

Then a rope dropped out of the sky. I stared, confused. It snaked around Lars and closed on him. Lars dropped his rifle with a startled cry. Then another polymer-plus lariat circled him and squeezed his arms to his side. He began to struggle.

"Yee-*haw!*" a familiar voice shouted. "We got that sucker!"

Joan and Deadshot were standing on the ridge, directly over Lars. They hauled on the rope and Lars' boots left the ground. The renegade dangled there, kicking and cursing.

I recovered the weapon he'd dropped. When Joan and Deadshot let Lars down, I stuck the barrel into his ribs. It would leave quite a hole if I fired it this close, I knew.

"Get over there, behind the rocks," I told him. "I've had just about enough from you!"

Lars did as I told him. Ziggy had him roped so fast, he might have been going for a rodeo championship. We didn't forget the switchblade in his boot, either.

Then I looked at Deadshot and Joan. "What are you doing here?" I called. I didn't care that they'd disobeyed my orders. They'd saved us and that was all that counted.

Deadshot said, "Why should you have all the fun?"

"But how did you do it?" I put my Master Time Belt back on. The others did the same.

"The colonel figured you were going to cancel the tour," Deadshot said. "Heck, we all figured it. So soon's you skedaddled, we sent Ziggy to keep an eye on you. He was supposed to keep you busy while we finished our dinosaur rodeo research."

I looked at Ziggy. He grinned and spread his arms.

"You needed me," he said.

"We spent another two weeks in the Cretaceous," Joan said, "roping and riding droms. Then we went back to the Jurassic just a few minutes after we'd left, so it would look like we'd been there all along. Only you and Ziggy didn't show."

"We were all tied up," I said.

Deadshot snorted. "Since you'd left all the info with the colonel, we decided to come looking. The others are on the other side of the pass. Lucky thing Joan and me heard them rifle shots!"

"You'd better go get the others," I told him. "We need to all be together, in case we have leave fast."

"Sure thing, Roy," he said. He turned and jogged out of sight. Then I heard him call, "Back in five minutes . . ."

Joan said, "What about those varmints out there?"

I looked where she was pointing. T.R. and Joe were still on their dinosaur-shooting spree, having too much fun to look back and see us.

"I don't know," I said.

"But the dinosaurs!" Mallory cried. "They're killing them like it's going out of style!"

"It *is* going out of style," Lars said. "Haven't you heard? The comet's going to strike soon, and they'll all be extinct anyway. So why worry about it?"

"There's something you don't know, Lars," Linda said. "The comet's coming down any minute now. My mother spent a lifetime figuring it out. She knew what she was talking about."

"Really?" Lars suddenly looked very nervous. He craned his neck to look at the sky. "Ha! That's a good one! I don't believe you."

"If you want," I said, "you stay here and find out for yourself. We'll just take a few holo-camera pictures and beat it back to the twenty-first century."

"Why hang around taking holo-pictures?" Joan asked. "Maybe we should just get out of here while we can."

"I promised Linda and Mallory they could," I said. "It means a lot to them."

"And we shouldn't leave Lars and his pals here," Mallory said.

"They should be brought in for trial," Joan said.

"They're trigger happy," Linda reminded us. "How can we bring them back? Especially with time running out the way it is?"

We all peered down at the plain. I counted three dozen alamosaurs lying on their sides, all dead or badly wounded. T.R. and Joe, looking like ants, circled the herd like vultures. The alamosaurs all huddled together, stamping their feet and looking confused. They didn't seem to connect their dead brothers with T.R. and Joe. As I watched, the two renegades aimed and fired again. Smoke came from their elephant guns' barrels. We heard the shots a few seconds later. Then another alamosaur slowly fell. I found a lump in my throat, and couldn't swallow it away.

"Leave them, Roy," Linda said. "The deserve whatever happens to them."

I knew it was a crazy thing to do, but for some reason I thought back to my Dad. He'd been left behind in the jaws of a Tyrannosaurus rex over a million years ago. Nobody deserved to die like that. Nobody deserved to die at all. I couldn't abandon these people, no matter how rotten they were.

"I'm going after them," I said quietly.

Chapter Twelve

I slung the laser rifle's strap over my shoulder and started down the slope toward the alamosaurus herd.

"Roy!"

I turned around to see Ziggy running after me. He caught up and grinned. "I won't let you go alone," he said.

"It's too dangerous," I said, deeply moved by what he was doing. "These men are killers, and the comet is going to come down any time now."

"Don't you think I know that?" he asked indignantly. "You're one of us now, Roy, and we stick together. Got it?"

I sighed. "Well, we're just wasting time standing here. Let's get going."

We started down the slope again, together, heading into the setting sun. The gunshots grew louder, and the alamosaurs grew ever more frantic. They honked and bleated and cried. And then they began to stampede, stirring up a huge cloud of dust.

Ziggy pulled a bandanna up over his mouth and nose, and made me do likewise. "You want to breathe, don't you?" he said.

"Yes!"

Then he asked, "Do you have a plan to sto them?"

"No. I just hope we can reason with them."

We entered the cloud of dust. It was thicke than I'd thought, and I found it hard to see. My eye began to water and sting. I blinked back tears. A around us, we could hear more gunshots and th honking of the alamosaurs.

Then I heard a roar. A very *familiar* roar tha stood the hairs on the back of my neck on end. felt cold all over, like winter had come and chille me to the bone. *I knew that roar!*

"T.R.! Help!" It was Joe's voice, plainly audibl in spite of the thunder of alamosaur feet. Joe's cr was followed by a scream, and then a gunshot.

"Come on!" Ziggy said.

We ran toward the sound.

A few seconds later, we almost bounced off th right foot of a Tyrannosaurus rex. It paid no atten tion to us, however, because it was busy eatin Joe.

I gasped. Ziggy moaned at the horrible sigh Joe, who had hoped to make his fortune in illeg dino-burgers, had become a meal for one of th creatures he stalked. It was a terrible, gruesom bloody vision. But appropriate.

I never thought I'd see another Tyrannosauru rex. I'd *prayed* never to see another one. I began t tremble all over. And then before I knew it, I raise my laser rifle and fired. And kept *on* firing.

I didn't hit the Tyrannosaur. But I could have if I'd wanted to, and that was enough for me.

"Come on!" Ziggy said, and pulled my arm.

Turning, I followed. Then, somewhere behind us, came another gunshot.

I looked back. The tyrannosaur suddenly had a wound on its left side. Dropping what was left of Joe, it threw back its head and roared that terrible roar.

It whirled on its attacker. Through a sudden swirl in the dust, I caught a glimpse of T.R. calmly reloading his elephant gun.

The tyrannosaur started toward him, still roaring in rage and pain. The dust cleared a little more. T.R. still had not moved. He showed no emotion. He calmly raised the elephant gun, aimed, and fired. This time he hit its head.

The tyrannosaur kept going like a train out of control. Then it collapsed, hitting the ground with a jolt.

Swirls of dust hid T.R. from us one second, and revealed him the next. He seemed not to notice us. Instead, he walked over to poor Joe and looked down at him for the last time.

T.R.'s eyes were haunted. Like many megalomaniacs, he probably hadn't ever thought such a thing could happen. He and his partners were the players, slaying these poor dumb brutes for profit, like ivory poachers in twentieth century Africa. But the tables had turned on Joe, and the same thing could happen to Time Runner Thompson.

"T.R., you've got to get out of here!" I shouted.

"The comet is going to hit right *here* any minute now!"

I don't think he understood me. If he did, he showed no sign of it. Instead, he reloaded his gun, turned, and darted off into the dust cloud. A few seconds later, he was gone.

"Hey!" Ziggy called after him. "You'll be killed!"

"T.R.!" I shouted.

When the dust cleared enough to see again, gunshots barked non-stop over the incessant roar of the alamosaur herd. I saw T.R. for only a moment. He was wading into the middle of the herd, reloading.

Then the herd changed direction. By the time he looked up, a twenty-meter-long alamosaur was barreling toward him, quite oblivious to the tiny human at its feet.

"No!" I cried.

Ziggy winced as the alamosaur trampled T.R. Thompson. The renegade vanished under its feet. I had no doubt he was dead; mercifully, dust obscured the awful sight. The predators had become the unwitting victims.

Ziggy and I started back across the plain, back the way we had come. The pass appeared a vast distance away. And it didn't seem to get any closer, though we were running as fast we we could. I couldn't even see Linda, Mallory, or Joan. But the rocks where the holo-camera was set up were visible.

We kept moving toward them. The dust was thinning out enough so that I finally caught a glimpse of our friends, minute figures waving us on and jumping up and down on the slope.

"We're going to make it!" I shouted.

"Yes!" Ziggy cried.

And that was when it happened.

Chapter Thirteen

The dinosaurs sensed it before the comet actually appeared. Of that much I'm certain. We were suddenly joined in our flight by all manner of them. An ornithomimus darted past us. A styracosaur rushed by, looking like a spiked rhinoceros. A tyrannosaur sprinted on its bird-of-prey talons. A pteranodon flapped overhead.

And then suddenly dinosaurs were all around us, running away from what could only have been the awesome thing we had come to see.

I glanced over my shoulder once, seeing Ziggy's frightened face. Behind him lay the sunset, red turning to pink turning to orange. The first stars of the evening twinkled. It would have been a lovely, tranquil sight, if it hadn't been for the frenzied stampede coming up behind us.

The alamosaurus herd had changed direction. They were heading toward the slope, too. A tiny mouselike animal darted into its hole. Every living thing was trying to get away.

I felt it too. Perhaps the comet's mass had begun to effect the Earth's gravity. Perhaps it was something else—a psychic warning of danger. I felt an electric current in the air, and the bright sunset seemed to suddenly turn a bit green. Then darkness fell over the land.

At that moment, I forgot about the stampeding dinosaurs, and even about the danger of being flattened by a comet. It had always been an abstraction before, but now—now it was really happening.

The comet split the sky. It was sudden, dramatic. I saw it as a tiny mote of brilliant light one moment, just one star among thousands. And then it began to swell toward gigantic proportions with alarming speed. Though I knew it was only supposed to be a little over fifteen kilometers in diameter, from where I stood it seemed to be big enough to swallow the Earth whole.

"Run!" I cried, and we fled before it. I kept glancing back as it grew larger and larger and larger. It took up most of the sky by the time we reached the slope.

We stumbled up to the two big rocks just in time. The colonel and everyone else was already there, watching with open mouths.

Ziggy and I turned to see, too. By the comet's glow, we saw hundreds, maybe *thousands* of dinosaurs fleeing for their lives. They swarmed through the pass to our left, heading for safety. The comet whizzed overhead, and the Earth seemed to swallow it. The western sky turned orange. That was the only effect, as far as I could tell.

"That's it?" Ziggy said, perplexed. "That's what all the excitement was about?"

"Well, shucks," said the colonel.

"Just wait," Linda said. She sat and pulled Mal- ry down beside her. "It hit several kilometers way. It's going to take time for the effects to reach ."

Then the whole sky lit up like it was noon. All a sudden, I heard a low rumble like thunder, only kept going on and on.

I crouched beside Linda, and everyone else und seats, too. In the distance, a gigantic fireball se into the air. I stared at it in awe for what emed hours.

Then the first shock-waves hit. They had to be reading out from the crater like ripples in a lake, realized later. But all I saw at the time were falling cks and bucking ground. I covered my head and ied to ride it out.

An immense fissure opened where the pass had een, not ten meters from where we lay. A struthio- imus, right leg caught on one side and left leg aught on the other, did the split, toppled, and fell eadlong into the chasm. Other dinosaurs, mostly amosaurs, followed it a second later, caught up in he mad rush to flee. They squealed as they fell.

When the chasm had filled with bodies, the inosaurs kept right on going. Wherever they came om, they were a teeming multitude of strange napes and sizes, all honking, hissing, roaring, and ellowing as they were tossed about by the shock aves.

Finally the ground settled enough to stand. The

sky was still orange; the comet had set off fires th
would rage for days, if not weeks. A huge pillar
smoke rose to the west.

It was overwhelming. Mallory clung to me an
I clung to her. We were both hoping the Eart
wouldn't open and swallow us the way it had swa
lowed so many dinosaurs in the pass. We were aliv
That was all that mattered now.

Suddenly cold, I shivered. Mallory shivered, to

"The sky," she said.

When I looked up, it seemed like a blanke
covered the world. The comet had thrown millior
of tons of dirt and dust into the stratosphere, I knev
The world would be a different place for man
years . . . cold and dark.

The age of the dinosaurs had come to a close.

"Wow," was all the colonel could say.

"Got your pictures?" I asked Linda.

She checked her camera, then nodded. "Got it.
Miraculously it hadn't fallen.

"Then let's get out of here before somethin
else happens."

"What about Joe and T.R.?" Lars demanded.

"I'm sorry," I said. "The dinosaurs got them."

It didn't take Linda and Mallory long to pac
up their holo-camera. By then everyone had ha
enough of the comet.

I glanced behind me only once more befor
shunting us home. Ash was falling from the sky lik
a heavy snowfall. Smoke and gasses released by th
comet had made the air almost unbreathable. I

wasn't a pretty world anymore. But it would be again, someday.

"Let's go home," I said. I set my Master Time Belt so it would include Lars's Time Belt, too, activated the override switch, and pushed the button.

Epilogue

Naturally we made it back safe and sound—just in the wrong place. When we arrived back home, we were standing in the middle of Main St. in Hogwallow, Texas. A couple of cars swerved to avoid us, horns honking. We had the good sense to get out of the street after that.

The colonel called taxis for all of us, and we rode back to the Time Tours building in air-conditioned luxury. Our drivers gave us some strange looks, but it was okay. The colonel tipped big.

A week later, everyone had been fully debriefed by the Time Patrol. The boys in black were none too happy with my actions as a Time Courier, and put several unkind comments in my file. But the colonel and his dino-punchers were pleased as punch with how everything turned out, and they made an even bigger stink about what a hero I was. Mallory even got it on all the network news shows. It seemed she still had some friends in show biz, after all. So all I got was an official slap on the wrist for my "eccentric acts." And stuck with a desk job for the next two months.

As a reward for capturing Lars (who was due for trial any day now), I got two months paid vacation ... which Louise let me take immediately.

The Texas Rodeo Association canceled its plans for a dinosaur rodeo, much to my surprise. It was a great idea, they said, but it would cost too much.

Oh, well. I didn't mind much. The colonel had promised me a job with his rodeo anytime I wanted one, and I planned on spending my vacation there with Ziggy and Joan and Deadshot and all the rest. Now that Ziggy had his new finger, he promised to teach me to rope and ride like a pro.

I don't know whether I have it in me to be a rodeo star, but I surely do intend to find out. I've had it with mind-tapes. From now on, *I'm* going to be one of those people making history.

And you know what? If this rodeo thing works out, I'm not coming back to work for the Time Service. At least, not till *I'm* ready for it, when I'm too old for bulldogging and riding and sharp-shooting. And that's going to be a *long* time.

Afterword
By Robert Silverberg

f there's going to be commercial time tourism, here's going to have to be a Time Patrol that makes certain that no one is able to change the past. There are no two ways about that. And a story about travelers who go back a hundred million year or so to see the dinosaurs in their natural habitat makes the Time Patrol's necessity absolutely clear:

Any change in the past will have consequences in times to come. And a change in the distant past, no matter how trivial, will have *tremendous* consequences as its effects widen and widen and widen in the course of spreading out over an immense period of time.

I first encountered this concept when I was a fourteen-year-old science-fiction reader, back in the late 1940s. It was in a story called "Brooklyn Project," by a sly and marvelous writer who used the name of "William Tenn." (His real name, I learned many years later, is Phil Klass, and he hasn't written any science fiction in many years, which is everybody's loss.)

I don't know if "Brooklyn Project" was the first

story to dramatize the startling consequences ⊙
making changes in the past—I doubt it—but it wa▸
and to this day remains, a wonderfully vivid an▸
dramatic demonstration of the theme. The Brookly▸
Project of the title is a reference to the code nam▸
for the development of the original atomic bom▸
during World War II. That was the Manhattan Pro▸
ect; and William Tenn's *Brooklyn* Project is pr▸
sented as yet another vast government scientifi▸
enterprise, this one intended to develop a workabl▸
system of travel through time. Ten billion dollar▸
and eight years of research have gone into the pro▸
ect—and now, as the story opens, a dozen reporter▸
are present at what is going to be the first larg▸
scale demonstration of successful time travel.

They are briefed on the background of the pro▸
ect, and then they ask reporterlike questions abou▸
the functions and appearance of the time-trave▸
apparatus. Culpepper of Consolidated News Servic▸
then asks the government spokesman about a recen▸
statement by a group calling itself the Federation ⊙
Chronar Scientists, warning that the experiment migh▸
be dangerous "because of insufficient data." Th▸
spokesman brushes the question aside. The Chrona▸
Scientists, he says, are simply traitors. There is n▸
reason to fear the experiment. Workable time trave▸
will be a magnificent weapon, which of course wil▸
be used only to preserve the peace. "Sending a▸
adequate mass of chronar into the past while it i▸
adjacent to a hostile nation would force that natio▸
into the future—all of it simultaneously—a futur▸

m which it would return populated only by
rpses!"

There are other, somewhat nervous, questions.
d then the experiment itself begins. A gong sounds,
d the chronar—the time probe—begins its jour-
y four billion years into the past.

"As you know," the spokesman says, "one of
e fears entertained about travel to the past was
at the most innocent-seeming acts would cause
taclysmic changes in the present." The traitorous
deration, he goes on, has maintained that even
ainor acts such as shifting a molecule of hydrogen
at in our past really never was shifted" could bring
out such changes. But preliminary tests have shown
at that is not so.

And now the chronar has reached its goal in
e past. A few drops of vapor condense from it and
l to the ground. The gong rings; the chronar
turns to the present, and sets out for the past
ain. Two billion years ago, now. "The great ball
cked its photographs of the fiery, erupting ground
low. Some red-hot crusts rattled off its sides. Five
six thousand complex molecules lost their basic
ucture as they impinged against it. A hundred
dn't."

And as the experiment goes on, the chronar
eates tiny impacts at each point in its journey: a
lobite is killed, then some bacteria, and so on.
e spokesman continues to address the reporters,
t what he says and does is somewhat different
ow. " '—will labor thirty hours a day out of thirty-
ree to convince you that black isn't white, that

we have seven moons instead of two,' " he declar
"slithering up and down rapidly now, gesturing w
all his pseudopods." And so on, until at last t
chronar is at rest. The experiment is over.

" 'See,' cried the thing that had been the acti
secretary to the executive assistant on press re
tions. 'See, no matter how subtly! Those who billo
were wrong: we haven't changed.' He extended
teen purple blobs triumphantly. 'Nothing h
changed!' "

I loved it. The gradual changes in reality, addi
up to an immense transformation—and the utt
unawareness of those who were being retroactive
transformed that anything was happening to them.

A few years later, in 1952, Ray Bradbury tackle
the same theme in his classic story, "A Sound
Thunder." Just as in our series of books, his sto
showed companies offering safaris into the past-
and, just as in *The Dinosaur Trackers*, Bradbury
travelers were heading back to the Mesozoic for
look at the giant reptiles. But there were risks,
Bradbury pointed out:

"A Time Machine is damn finicky business. N
knowing it, we might kill an important animal,
small bird, a roach, a flower, even, thus destroyi
an important link in a growing species. . . . Say w
accidentally kill one mouse here. That means
the future families of this one particular mouse a
destroyed. And all the families of the families of th
families of that one mouse! With a stamp of you
foot, you annihilate first one, then a dozen, then
thousand, a million, a *billion* possible mice!"

What about the fox that dies because there are
no mice for it to eat? The lion that starves because
there are no foxes? The changes that take place
because the lion isn't there to hunt its prey? And so
on and so on and so on, until "the stamp of your
boot, on one mouse, could start an earthquake, the
effects of which could shake our Earth and destinies
down through Time, to their very foundations. With
the death of one cave man, a billion others yet
unborn are throttled in the womb. Perhaps Rome
never rises on its seven hills. Perhaps Europe is
forever a dark forest. . . ."

Step on a mouse and you crush the Pyramids,
Bradbury says. Crush a blade of grass and you may
create a vast famine millions of years later. *Be careful. Don't change the past.*

When I created my own time-tour industry for
my novel *Up the Line* in 1968, I had "Brooklyn
Project" and "A Sound of Thunder" and dozens of
other don't-mess-with-the-past stories in mind. But I
had to make my own adjustments to the problems
of time paradoxes if I was going to be able to tell
my story.

(I need to remind you here and I don't actually
and literally believe that we're going to have commercial time tours running in the near future, or
ever at all, for that matter. The scientific side of my
mind has trouble swallowing the basic concept of
easy travel back and forth in time. But *for the sake
of the story* I have no trouble at all making believe
that time travel is technically possible. If science-
fiction writers weren't able to make imaginative

jumps of that sort, the only science fiction that would get written would be very dull stuff indeed.)

I couldn't, for example, accept William Tenn's "Brooklyn Project" hypothesis, charming as it is, at all. It's simply too extreme. If even the slightest chemical change in the past is going to have colossal consequences farther on down the line, then no time travel at all can be permitted, for there's no way to isolate time travelers completely from the environment of the past. They'd have to breathe; they'd be walking around, transferring modern molecules to the soil with every step they took; and so forth. Even if we put them inside sealed chambers, there'd be chemical reactions between the outsides of those chambers and the atmosphere of the past. I couldn't work within limits like that—though I was glad Tenn had, in his very funny story.

Bradbury's restrictions were also too severe. Crush a single blade of grass and the future will change? In his story, the time travelers are required to keep strictly to a prescribed path. Stepping off the path is prohibited. Someone does, and steps on a butterfly, and the whole future is changed.

Again, a great story, but too restrictive a situation. My time tourists are *bound* to kill a few bugs, and more, wherever they go. If changes that small will transform the future, then no one can be allowed to go into the past.

My response was to declare that minor changes didn't matter. As one of my Time Couriers explains to a new recruit, "As you get into this business, Jud, you'll find out that we're in constant intersection with past events. Every time a Time Courier steps on an ant in 2000 B.C., he's changing the past. Somehow we survive." The Time Patrol watches out for major changes—*structural* changes, such as making sure that Julius Caesar stayed home on the Ides of March, or giving Alexander the Great antibiotics when he lay dying of some internal infection at the age of 33. "They leave the little crap alone. They have to. There aren't enough patrolmen to handle everything."

To which the young recruit replies, "But that means that we're building up a lot of tiny alterations in history, bit by bit, an ant here and a butterfly there, and the accumulation may someday cause a major change, and nobody will then be able to trace all the causes and put things back the way they ought to be!"

"Exactly."

"You don't sound worried about it."

"Why should I be? Do I own the world?" the older Time Courier says.

A cynical response from a cynical man—but in the world of my *Up the Line,* at any rate, they all get away with it. Minor changes in the past create no problems, and major interferences in the established flow of history are quickly canceled out by a Time Patrol that ranges freely from one end of time to the other, standing outside the effect-zone of the changes. Of course, what might be a minor interference a hundred and fifty years back—shooting one of the millions of bison that roamed the American West at that time—might be a gigantic interference in the Mesozoic, considering how many millions of years separate that era from our own and how great the widening ramifications of the change might become. That far back, the Patrol would have to keep unusually close watch on the travelers. But stepping on the occasional blade of grass—the true grasses probably hadn't evolved yet in the Mesozoic, by the way—probably wouldn't make all that much difference, is my guess.

Which is right? My notion that only the big changes count, or Ray Bradbury's view that the death of one mouse can keep the Roman Empire from happening?

I don't know. Nobody does. We aren't really very likely to find out.

But I do know that if time tourists ever do start wandering around freely through the epochs behind us, I want to see a tough, no-nonsense Time Patrol on duty. Just to make certain that those of us who stay home don't wind up burbling and billowing and waving our fifteen purple blobs around.

DATABANK

Time Services thoroughly researches a time period before opening it up to tourists. Research historians are sent back to study, map, photograph, tape, and record every aspect of life in a past era. Only when their work is finished do the Time Tours begin.

All hypnosleep courses for tourists (and Couriers) are prepared based on fully accurate notes and recordings. Time Services is proud of its 99.98 percent accuracy rate in charting past events.

Before you take your Age of Reptiles tour, you may view files on dinosaurs such as the TARBOSAURUS and DEINONYCHUS. Pay attention to the specialized equipment such as the H.I.B. LASER RIFLE and the DOME DURO-TENT; remember, this is a dangerous era.

Be sure to report to the Time Tours Travel Station promptly, and be sure that everything you bring into the past has been approved by your Time Courier.

Dinosaur Riding

One of the biggest lures for cowboys is the Mesozoic, where dinosaurs like the dromiceiomimus—or droms—can be roped and ridden. The droms were the swiftest of all dinosaurs, and could outrun a horse.

DEINONYCHUS

Length: 2.4–4 meters (8–14 feet)
Height: Approx. 2 meters (6.5 feet)

Two Deinonychuses Face Off

The Deinonychus, or "terrible claws," are the most dangerous flesh-eating dinosaurs of the early Cretaceous period. They were among the fastest, fiercest, and most intelligent hunters of their time. They sometimes hid in ambush, waiting for prey, or hunted in large packs. Tourists should keep well under cover while observing this species of dinosaur.

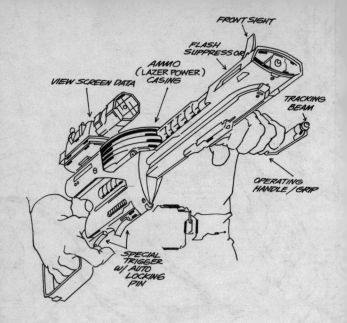

FRONT SIGHT

FLASH SUPPRESSOR

AMMO (LAZER POWER) CASING

VIEW SCREEN DATA

TRACKING BEAM

OPERATING HANDLE / GRIP

SPECIAL TRIGGER w/ AUTO LOCKING PIN

H.I.B. Laser Rifle

This High Intensity Beam rifle is used for protection against larger creatures—dinosaurs, for example. Target beam and tracking scope plus ten settings allow maximum control.

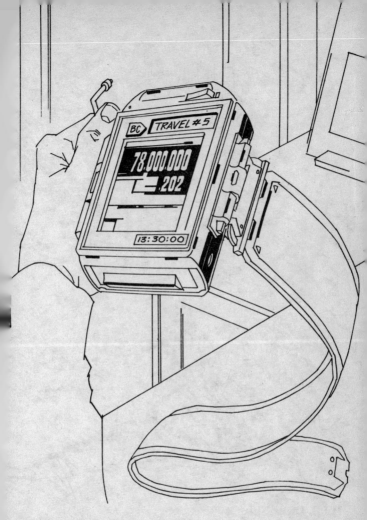

The Time Belt

The Time Belt is the prime mechanism of the Time Tourist. The Time Courier wears a Master Time Belt, which automatically resets the timers in each tourist's belt. This one is set for 78 million years, B.C., February 2, 1:30 P.M. (78,000,000.202 13:30:00).

Two Dinosaurs of the Cretaceous Period (136–65 million years ago)

TARBOSAURUS

Length: 10–14 meters (33–46 feet)
Height: 4.5–6.0 meters

PARASAUROLOPHUS WALKERI

Length: 10 meters (33 feet)
Height: Approx. 4.5 meters (13 feet)

The Dome Duro-Tent

The Time Service uses the most rugged equipment possible during tours. The Dome Duro-Tent is constructed of kevlar, a nearly indestructible fabric, which can be compressed into a cylinder 15.5 centimeters (about 6 inches) long. Lighting, heating, and cooling systems are built into the tent structure. Here we see Mallory and Roy at the campsite.

IT'S THE ULTIMATE
IN VERSIMILITUDE!
THE HOUSTON TIME
TOUR BANCH BRINGS
YOU TO THE PAST
FASTER~~~LONGER~~~
BETTER~~~AND FOR
LESS! SATISFACTION
GUARANTEED! NO
EON TOO BIG~~~NO
INCIDENT TOO SMALL!
ASK ABOUT OUR
FREQUENT TRAVELER
DISCOUNT PLAN!
DON'T LEAVE
THE PRESENT
WITHOUT
US!

Time Tours Travel Station

*The Houston Time Tours Travel Station is seventy stories
high and sports the largest neon sign ever constructed.*